Murder Is Universal
A Susan Wiles Schoolhouse Mystery

by

Diane Weiner

For information, email Cozy Cat Press, cozycatpress@aol.com or visit our website at: www.cozycatpress.com

COZY CAT
P R E S S

ISBN: 978-1-952579-06-6
Printed in the United States of America

10 9 8 7 6 5 4 3 2 1

Acknowledgements

Special thanks to my editor, Laura Grigull, whose attention to detail is second to none, and to my reader, Janalyn, for her insights into writing the fictional character who shares her name in this book. And as always, thanks to my publisher, Patricia Rockwell, whose dedication and support have made my dream of becoming an author a reality.

Chapter 1

"Excuse me." Susan Wiles tugged her travel bag and her overflowing purse over the portly passenger in the middle seat. Stuck. She cleared her throat and repeated herself.

Glaring at her with his arrogant blue eyes, the balding, middle-aged man in the tweed jacket grabbed the back of the seat in front of him and hoisted himself up.

"The bag needs to go in the overhead bin. It won't fit under the seat. Didn't you look at the visual at check-in?" Huffing and grumbling, he stepped into the aisle while she jammed the bag into the space in front of her feet and clicked her seatbelt.

Clutching her purse on her lap, she felt his elbow jab her arm as he plopped back down. Her sandal-clad feet kicked against the bag yearning to stretch, but with her stubby legs, it was impossible. *I should have paid for extra leg room. Before you know it, the nickel and diming airlines will be charging us for oxygen.*

Her new bestie, Valerie, sat in the aisle seat and immediately commanded the arm rest. Her waist overflowed under it despite the ten pounds she'd lost since following the *Lazy Vegetarian* plan she and Susan started after first meeting in St. Louis a few months ago.

As soon as they were airborne for LaGuardia, Susan whipped out the chocolate covered almonds she'd purchased in the candy store at the St. Louis airport and offered some to Valerie, reaching over the middle passenger.

"Thanks." Valerie held out her palm and chuckled "No animals were killed making these, right?"

The man in the middle huffed. "Wouldn't you like to trade seats with me so you can talk to your friend?"

"Sit in the dreaded middle? No, thanks," said Valerie, continuing the conversation over him. "Do you think your realtor friend can find a house Jazzy and I can afford?"

"The new community where my father lives would be perfect for the three of you. And I know some of the teachers at the school Elijah would be attending."

"My daughter is pretty darn fussy. She'll want to know if the neighborhood is," she cleared her throat, '*diverse.*' She doesn't want Elijah going to some all-white suburban school."

Susan mentally pictured her chorus the year she retired—two African-Americans, one Asian, and a handful of Jewish kids. "Westbrook isn't St. Louis." She left it at that.

The man in the middle struggled to get his laptop out of its case, then plopped it on the tray table. Susan and Valerie continued chatting over him.

"Is Mike back to work yet?"

"He's going in a few hours a day. We're trying to figure out our finances." Susan looked at the man's laptop screen, noticed the university logo, and said, "SUNY Westbrook? My son-in-law teaches there. Jason Greene. Maybe you know him? He's married to my daughter."

"No, really? Your son-in-law is married to your daughter?"

"No need to be sarcastic. These days he could just as easily be married to my son."

She whipped out her phone. "These are their children. That's Annalise and the little one's Mia. They adopted her from China."

"I don't give a …" The man sighed. "I have a lot of work to do, if you don't mind. Are you sure you don't want to trade places?"

"No, thanks. I paid extra for this seat." She patted the arm rest. After a few minutes, Susan undid her seatbelt and reached in front of her for the travel bag. She bent down, rattled the man's laptop, and bumped his tray while trying to wriggle her magazine out of her bag. The man steadied it only to have it jarred a second time when Susan reached down to retrieve her bifocals.

"I give up." The man slammed the lid down on the laptop. He took a tiny burlap bag from his satchel, and with his thick fingers, tugged at a red string to open it.

Valerie gasped. "Is that Snacky Sax? I see them everywhere. They're more popular than ice cream in July." She sniffed. "Smells like coconut. Is it good?"

The man snatched the bag out of her reach, swallowed a handful, and muttered something about giving up. Then, he covered his ears with the padded earphones he pulled from his bag.

Susan read for a while, then felt her eyes winning the fight to close. When she woke up, head against the window, the lights of New York City twinkled below. Minutes later, the plane thumped onto the runway and braked to a hard stop. Susan undid her seatbelt and stood up waiting for their turn to exit. The man in the middle was asleep. She said, "Excuse me. We're here." He didn't budge. "I said, we've landed."

She turned to Valerie. "Should I shake him or what?"

"Unless you want us to be the last ones off."

Susan shook him. His head flopped over. She shook him harder, accidentally brushing her hand against his cold cheek. "Sir? Are you okay?" She noticed his chest wasn't moving in and out and her pulse quickened. "He's not breathing. Get the flight attendant." Trapped next to the window, her heart pounded and she grabbed the airsick bag out of the seat pocket just in case.

"No one's going to let me cut in." Valerie put her hand in front of his nose. "Oh my God. Is he...dead? He can't be dead."

"Did you see anything odd while I was asleep?"

"I got up to use the restroom and by the time I came back he was fast asleep."

A line of passengers with the single goal of exiting the plane, tugged bags from the overhead bins and pushed toward the exit not noticing any of this.

"Go get help!" Susan shouted into the aisle. "We have a medical emergency. Let my friend through!"

She was afraid Valerie was going to faint, but she pulled herself together and squirmed into the aisle. Susan said a quick prayer. By the time Valerie returned with a flight attendant, the plane had emptied.

Minutes later, paramedics stormed onto the plane. Trapped between the passenger and the window, Susan noticed a blue tinge circling the passenger's lips and the contents of his half-eaten snack bag spilled onto the floor below.

The flight attendant addressed the paramedics. "I'll bet he had a heart attack. Is he okay?"

Susan had witnessed her husband's two heart attacks and wasn't convinced.

The paramedics worked to revive him. As far as Susan could tell, they were unsuccessful. When they finally extracted the poor man from his seat and wheeled him away, Susan was able to get out into the aisle.

Valerie, who'd been standing in the row behind them, whispered in Susan's ear. "Poor man."

She felt nauseated. *Why the blue lips?* Her intuition told her there was more to this man's death than a heart attack.

Chapter 2

In the morning, Susan smelled coffee as she padded down the steps and into the kitchen. Mike was scrambling up breakfast at the stove. Visiting Evan in St. Louis was always a treat but it was good to be home. Heaven knows, she never could figure out how to work Evan's bean grinding, barista robot of a coffee maker. She scooped up Johann, nuzzling his fur.

Mike looked over his shoulder. "Hey, are you okay? You were pretty rattled when I picked you up from the airport. And I felt you tossing and turning half the night."

"Seeing a dead body isn't easy—even when it's not the first time."

"Want some gourmet egg whites and whole wheat toast?" Mike gave her a kiss as she pulled a mug from the cabinet.

"So you've been following your diet the whole time I was gone?"

"With the exception of a sausage pizza the other night, yeah. Should I scramble up some for Valerie, or is she still asleep?"

"The guest room door was still shut. We've got an appointment with the realtor in an hour. Jazmin's depending on her mom to get something lined up quickly so when she takes over as Lynette's partner she'll hit the ground running."

"And you'll have your new best friend in town."

She smiled at the thought. "Remember, we've got the going away party for Jackson and Theresa tonight."

She spotted the newspaper on the table. "Anything about the dead passenger in there?"

"Haven't had a chance to look. I know it freaked you out, him having a heart attack right next to you. Especially after what happened last spring."

"I'm not buying the heart attack."

"Not again." He scooped eggs onto the plate and sighed. "Let's hear it."

She leaned closer. "If someone's having a heart attack, they have pain, right? You've been through it. You told me you felt like an elephant sat on your chest. You didn't simply nod off quietly."

"But everyone's different."

"And your lips didn't turn blue."

"I don't know. It's not like I checked in the mirror. Where's that coming from?"

"Something I noticed while we waited for the paramedics. And he ate one of those Snacky Sax right before. Half of it wound up on the floor."

"So someone snuck up on him and threw a poisoned sack of snacks into his bag to kill him?"

"Snacky Sax. Not sack of snacks." She leafed through the paper. "Here's a story. Harold Chambers, of Succex college prep fame, died while returning to Westbrook after attending a college showcase conference in St. Louis." She shouted, "That's the conference Jason was supposed to go to before Mia got sick and he had to cancel."

"I know. I was in the room when he gave you his ticket."

"This guy had his laptop open and I saw the SUNY Westbrook logo. I thought maybe he was a professor but he didn't want to talk to us so I wasn't certain." She heard Valerie's footsteps coming down the stairs.

Valerie came into the kitchen. "Certain of what?" She smiled at Mike. "I mean, good morning. Are those for me?"

"Yep." He scooped eggs onto a plate and handed it to her. "Did you sleep well?"

"Sure did. I had a furry little friend keeping me company."

"Ludwig," said Susan. "He loves to cuddle. And the one on the window ledge enjoying the morning sun is Johann."

"Did I hear you talking about the guy who was murdered last night?"

Mike said, "No one's calling it murder. There's an article in the paper. Says he died of natural causes."

"Hah," said Valerie. "Natural causes my foot. Blue lips? Someone poisoned his candy, that's what I think. Just wait till your daughter gets her hands on the case and you'll see."

Susan nodded. "I wonder if Jason knew him. Guess I'll find out tonight."

Mike tossed the rest of his coffee in the sink. "I'll be home around 4:00. Good luck house hunting." He grabbed his lunch box on his way out.

"I'm anxious to see the town," said Valerie. She pushed the food around on her plate.

"You're not eating your egg whites."

"Neither are you."

"We'll drive through Starbucks on the way and get muffins."

They headed for the real estate office.

Susan's neighborhood, mostly retirees with families raised and mortgages paid off, had been built in the late 70's. The spindly trees that lined the fresh sidewalks when they first moved in had blossomed into a canopy of plush trees, vivid green in summer but fired with color during the fall. About this time every summer, with the afternoon thunderstorms and sauna-like humidity, Susan dreamed of cool, crisp, sweater weather. She could almost taste it refreshing her nasal passages.

Valerie plastered her nose to the passenger side window, drinking in the new surroundings. "I like your neighborhood. Not zero lot lines, but not so spread out you lack neighbors."

"We've been happy here. Of course, the houses are older. We had to install central air some years ago. Thank goodness we did. On a day like today we'd be melting."

They drove past the new shopping mall and into downtown where Susan parallel parked in front of a brick real estate office. A bell tingled when they entered, and they were greeted by a woman in her early fifties, wearing a linen pantsuit.

"Mrs. Wiles, I'm glad you called."

"My father loves living at La Puebla so I thought of you. This is my friend, Valerie Holmes. Like I said on the phone, her daughter and grandson will be moving here within the month and they need a place that can accommodate all three."

"And not too expensive," added Valerie. "I'm on a fixed income and the police department ain't covering our moving expenses."

"We've got some good options." She pulled out a map and pointed with her French-manicured finger. "We're here. And this is Susan's father's neighborhood. There are a few new homes still for sale." She looked away for a moment. "You know, I just thought of something." She slid her finger across the map. "There's an older community halfway between here and La Puebla. A cute three-bedroom just went on the market yesterday and it's a steal. If you're interested, we can take a look."

"Sure. Let's get started." Valerie followed Susan into the agent's car.

While waiting for the air to kick in, Susan fanned herself with a coupon booklet she'd picked up on the way out of the office. The neon sign over the bank they passed showed a temperature of 90 degrees, and with the Hudson Valley's August humidity, her back felt damp against the car seat.

The agent drove them down a wide, tree-lined street. "That's the university on the left. Beautiful homes but they cost a fortune. The founder of Succex lives right there. You know Succex, right? The college prep company." She pointed at a yellow wooden house with a wrap-around porch and weeping willows in the front yard. "Guess I should have said lived. Of course, you heard what happened."

"Heard? He sat between us on the plane yesterday," said Susan.

"No way."

"I swear."

"At least his trophy wife will be taken care of. The house was paid off years ago and that company's worth a fortune. I wonder if she's planning on selling or running the business herself. Then again, why work if you don't have to." She spoke into her Apple watch. "Reminder to contact Chambers' widow about selling."

Valerie said, "What sort of business is it? College prep. What's that mean?"

The agent answered, "My sister used them for my nephew. Cost an arm and a leg but my brother-in-law is a surgeon so they could afford it. My sister never had to work a day in her life, but that's another story. They offer tutoring for the SAT's, help write college essays, and recommend colleges. My nephew got into Brown. They advertise a 95% placement rate."

Susan stuck the damp coupon book in her purse. "I'll bet they're choosey about who they take into the program in the first place."

The agent shrugged her shoulders. "Probably." She turned into a tree-lined community and chirped as if on autopilot, "What I like about this neighborhood is how each house has its own character. None of that cookie cutter architecture that's so common nowadays. Look to your left. See the 'For Sale' sign? It'll be gone by tomorrow if it isn't already. Lovely, right?"

Valerie said, "It's… big. Let's see inside before I make a judgment."

"Shady trees. It'll keep the electric bills down on days like today." The agent opened the lock box. "It gets the morning sun so later in the day the living room stays cooler."

They walked into a cavernous living room with hard wood floors that melted into a dining room and then a spacious kitchen.

Valerie opened the cabinets and the appliances. "The stove looks like it's in mint condition."

"All the appliances are new. The owners put them in recently."

"Then they left? Where'd they go?" asked Valerie.

The agent shrugged her shoulders. "I don't know. Some sort of emergency. They were anxious to sell." She opened a slatted, accordion door next to the refrigerator. "The laundry room is here." Then she walked across the kitchen. "The third bedroom's in here. Downstairs. Nice and private if you're planning on living with your daughter."

Susan whispered in Valerie's ear. "You can sneak in guys and Jazmin will never be the wiser."

Valerie gave her a light push, then walked into the bedroom and examined the bathroom and closet.

"Looks like plenty of room for my furniture and exercise bike."

"Come see the back yard." The agent pulled opened a sliding glass door. "You've got this patio to barbecue on and the grass area is plenty big. The owners installed the swing set for their kid. And looks like they left behind a brand new wading pool."

They walked out onto the lawn where Valerie examined the swings. "This looks brand new." Valerie ran her hand along the seat. "And expensive."

Susan gave the swing a push. "Why put this in if you planned on moving?"

The agent hurried them inside. "We've got the place in La Puebla to look at as well. Are you ready?"

"I'd like to see upstairs," said Valerie. The staircase was immediately to the right of the front door. She climbed up and wandered into the master bedroom. "This is nice. Jazzy'd have room to set up a little office in here. She's always working, even when she's at home."

"And follow me." The realtor led them to a bedroom across the hall with pale blue walls. "The father put those cute little stars on the ceiling. They light up at night."

"Elijah, my grandson, loves anything to do with outer space. He dressed up like an astronaut last Halloween."

"How old is he?"

"He turned eight last month."

"Did I mention there's a park down the road? And the school bus stop is right across the street."

"How much are they asking?"

The agent pulled out the paperwork. "Like I said, it's a steal. Less than the places in La Puebla and twice the amount of space. It's going to go fast."

"I'm going to talk to Jazzy right away. I think we found our new home."

Chapter 3

Susan and Valerie relaxed until it was time to get ready for the going away party. Mike shouted up the staircase over the late afternoon thunderstorm. "Susan, are you about ready? The party is supposed to be a surprise. We have to get there before Teresa and Jackson."

"I'm coming." She padded down the steps in white cotton pants and a button-down floral blouse. "Valerie will be down in a minute."

"How'd the house-hunting go?"

"I think she found their dream home. She was on the phone most of the afternoon with her daughter."

Valerie came downstairs. "I sent Jazzy the photos from the realtor and she's checking out her finances. If everything lines up, she thinks she'll make an offer."

"She must really trust you," said Mike.

"She does."

"Hope it works out." Mike grabbed his keys and an umbrella from the hall table. "We'd better go or we'll be late."

Their daughter, Lynette, and hubby Jason lived near the university. When they arrived, the house was alive with laughter and the aroma of lasagna and garlic bread filled the air. Pint-sized Annalise with her new sandals and gingham sundress, ran up to Susan, arms outstretched.

"Pick me up, Grandma." Susan covered her with kisses. "Delicious. I missed you. I brought you a present."

"What is it?"

Susan pulled a stuffed bear from her purse. "It says St. Louis. That's…"

"In Missouri. Where Uncle Evan lives."

Valerie said, "Aren't you a brilliant little angel. Look at those silky blond braids. When Jazzy was little, I used to use up a whole package of hair bands doing her corn rows."

Lynette said, "I heard a car. Everyone hide." She turned out the lights. When the bell rang, she opened the door to shouts of "surprise."

Theresa held their squirmy son, Ian. "Oh, my God. I didn't expect this. I thought it was just us for dinner."

Jason wriggled Mia to one side and grabbed a bottle of wine from Jackson.

Jackson, pudgy with a prematurely receding hairline, tucked in his polo shirt where it had been pulled out when he struggled to get Ian out of the car seat. "Wow, this is awesome, everyone. You're gonna make it hard to leave."

Susan introduced Valerie. "Her daughter, Jazmin, is going to be Lynette's partner."

"I heard all about Detective Lowe from Lynette," said Jackson. "She's happy to replace me."

Lynette swatted his arm. "Not true. I'm going to miss you both but the new job is a promotion and you'll only be a few hours away."

Jackson nodded. "And the raise will be appreciated. Especially with the new baby on the way."

"What!" Susan squealed.

"Congratulations." Lynette and Susan took turns hugging him.

Susan said to Ian, "You're going to be a big brother. Won't it be fun to have someone to play with?"

Ian started to cry.

Jason said, "Let's eat. Buffet style. Grab a plate. Lasagna's Lynette's specialty."

Susan fixed a plate, then sat on the sofa with Valerie and Mike.

Susan eyed Jason, Mia in tow, and watched Lynette, who juggled two plates as she struggled to sit down. Sometimes she felt nostalgic for the days when the kids were growing up; other days she felt thankful those days were past, wondering how she ever had the energy to keep up with active Lynette and ever curious Evan.

What started as a conversation about Lynette's garlic bread recipe, ended up as speculations and theories about the dead passenger.

Jason said, "I work with Harold Chambers' wife at the university. Her office is next to mine. Poor woman. This must be hitting her hard."

"Especially since he didn't die of natural causes," said Susan.

"Mom, what are you talking about? The man had a heart attack."

"You'll see. I noticed his lips were blue. And he didn't act like a man having a heart attack. I know. I've been through it twice with your father."

Lynette rolled her eyes at her. "Here we go again. Did you check out the Zumba classes I told you about? Or the book club at the senior center?"

Officer Rob McGinnis, from Lynette's department, sat down. "I wouldn't be surprised if she's right. The guy had lots of enemies."

Lynette said, "What are you talking about?"

"My son—straight A average, captain of the track team and state debate champion, was turned down by Harvard."

"That's a very competitive school," said Jason.

"But one of his much less qualified classmates who attended Succex got in. Sean White. The kid had to drop out of AP Calculus because he couldn't cut it, and took the SAT's two or three times. He wasn't even in the top ten percent of his class but his Daddy is rich and Chambers got the kid got in."

Susan said, "That's terrible."

"There's no way I could have sent my son to that stuck up prep program on my cop's salary, but I know someone who probably took out a second mortgage on his nursery business to send his kid. Bruno Vitulli had the same credentials as my son Tyler and didn't get in. Carmine, the father, threatened to kill Chambers right in the middle of a track meet. Everyone in the bleachers heard him."

Susan couldn't help picturing Annalise in the same shoes as Officer McGinnis's son. Surely she'd be bright enough for an Ivy League school, but Lynette and Jason were far from rich. The imagined injustice bubbled in her veins.

Jason said, "This is supposed to be a pleasant send-off for our friends. Let's talk about something else."

"How about cake?" said Annalise. "Mommy and I baked a cake for Aunt Theresa and Uncle Jacky. We doubled the recipe. Baking powder makes the cake rise."

Valerie turned to Annalise. "How old are you?"

Annalise held up five fingers.

Stuffed on lasagna, Susan checked her sugar level before indulging in cake. She'd been able to control her type 2 diabetes with diet alone the past few months, but she'd been a bit lax lately, especially with traveling.

Theresa said, "How are your son's wedding plans going?"

"They're looking into a destination wedding since residents get limited vacation time. Nothing solid yet."

"Did you get your mother-of-the groom dress?"

"I want to lose a few pounds first. Did I tell you Annalise is going to be the flower girl? She's so excited. She's been practicing dropping petals. The lilac bush outside is looking bare."

Officer McGinnis balanced a plate of cake and a cup of coffee. "You know the guy I was telling you about? The one who threatened to kill Harold Chambers?"

Susan set down her cake. "Yes, do you think he's a suspect?"

"You said the guy had blue lips, right?"

"Yes, as in poisoning."

"Mom, stop that. And Rob, stop encouraging her."

"When you get the report from the medical examiner you'll see I was right." She turned back to Rob McGinnis. "Why do you ask?"

"He died after eating candy?"

"Snacky Sax."

"Hmm."

"Does that mean something to you?"

"It's just...the guy I was talking about owns a nursery. Cyanide is known for turning lips and nails blue. I'm no expert, but isn't cyanide found in pesticides? And in pits from certain fruits?"

"Peaches, I think. Or maybe that's arsenic."

"He's got a bunch of fruit trees out there. And although I like the guy, he is a bit of a hot head. I don't know, it's a gut feeling, not that I'd blame him. That's the cop in me." Lynette shot him a look. "Forget I mentioned it. We don't even know if he was poisoned yet and even if he was, it could have been accidental."

"Whoever did it had to have access to plant the poison, either on this end or in St. Louis."

"Well, one step at a time. For now, it's a case of death by natural causes and if it turns out to be murder, I can't be discussing it."

Susan was sure that was for Lynette, his superior's, benefit.

"I understand. So where is your son going to college?"

"Right here at SUNY Westbrook."

"A great reputation and a quarter the price of an Ivy League school."

"I know. He'd do well wherever he goes. I'm going to get a second piece of cake."

Jackson wandered over. "I hope Lynette warns her new partner you love to meddle in police business."

"Hah. I thought we'd reached an understanding. I thought you'd come to regard me more as a consultant, especially when there was a school connection."

"I have to admit you were somewhat helpful. When you didn't overstep your bounds."

"You're going to miss me. And I'll miss you, too. You always had my daughter's back."

"All in a day's work. Theresa's parents live here and with two grandchildren, we'll be coming by to visit often." He gave her a hug. "Ian's getting cranky. We're going to be taking off."

Jackson and Theresa made the rounds with their goodbyes. Susan noticed Valerie yawning and she herself felt her eyes getting heavy.

Mike said, "Want to go? I have work tomorrow."

Susan agreed. "Valerie and I have some work to do tomorrow, too."

Mike cleared his throat. "You mean in regards to the new house, right?"

"Um, sure. That's exactly what I meant."

Chapter 4

The next morning, Susan and Valerie had barely finished breakfast when Lynette called.

"Hi, honey. Lovely party last night. Isn't it great news about the new baby?"

"Yes. Great news. Mom, can you and Valerie come down to the station?"

"Is everything okay?"

"Yeah. I wanted to ask a few questions about Harold Chambers. You and Valerie were the last two people to see him alive."

She found out it was murder and now she wants my help. "I knew I was right. We'll be right over." She hung up before Lynette could respond.

Susan turned to Valerie. "We were right. It was murder and *now* Lynette wants our help."

She shuddered. "Creepy, ain't it? One minute the guy is talking to us and the next he's dead."

"Yeah. His poor wife. She'd have been expecting him home after a couple of days. She'll never see him again."

Valerie said, "Yeah. I can't imagine. Give me ten minutes and I'll be ready."

Valerie's eyes were glued to the passenger window, absorbing the sights along the short drive to the police station.

When they got to the station, Susan felt a twinge in the pit of her stomach when she passed by Jackson's empty office. *It's for the best for his soon to be family of four. Especially since Theresa plans to take a break from teaching while the kids are young. I don't know how parents do it these days. Two kids in daycare? Lynette and Jason are counting the days until fall when Annalise starts kindergarten and they'll only be paying for one child.*

Valerie said, "The station is a lot smaller than the station back in St. Louis. And cleaner."

"Well, you said one of the reasons this job attracted Jazzy was she'd be raising Elijah in a small town rather than the city. Come on. This is Lynette's office." She knocked on the door.

"Come in." Lynette's desk was piled with messy folders and loose papers that immediately struck Susan as weird. Lynette was a 'place for everything and everything in its place' kind of girl. Ever since she was little. She'd even trained Annalise to organize her dolls by height order on her shelf.

"Looks like you've got your hands full."

"I'm working all Jackson's open cases as well as the ones we were doing together *and* there was a robbery last night."

"Jazzy will be here soon to help," said Valerie.

"I need her yesterday. Anyway, turns out the snack Harold Chambers ate was laced with cyanide. Did you notice anything unusual while you were on the plane with him?"

Susan said, "I told you about the blue lips."

"Besides that."

"He had his laptop open and I saw the logo for SUNY Westbrook."

Valerie chimed in. "He wasn't friendly. Not one for small talk. I noticed he had a couple of bags of snacks tucked in his laptop case. Not that he needed to be eatin' with that big old gut of his."

"When did you first notice he was…dead?"

Valerie said, "I thought he was asleep. He'd put on those pillowy headphones and closed his eyes. Susan fell asleep and I was watching a movie on my phone. Then I got up to use the restroom. I didn't notice anything wrong until we landed and he didn't get up."

"I smelled almonds," said Susan. "But I figured it was from the snack he was eating."

Valerie said, "To be truthful, your mother and I were eating chocolate covered almonds when we first got on the plane."

"Did you see him eat or drink anything besides the Snacky Sax? Or take medication?"

"No."

"Did he make any calls or act agitated?"

"No," said Valerie. "Annoyed, maybe, but not agitated. We were trying to be hospitable."

"Rob McGinnis at your party last night said Harold Chambers had enemies. Didn't you hear him say a father on his kid's track team threatened to kill him over his son not getting into Harvard?"

"We'd need more than an idle threat to put someone on the suspect list. If you think of any other details, call me."

"Of course." Susan loved feeling useful, especially since retiring a few years ago.

Her bifocals fogged up as soon as they left the building and stepped into the humidity. She cranked up the AC as soon as they got into the car. She'd barely left the parking lot when her phone buzzed.

"Hey, Jason. What? Sure. I'll run by and get it."

"Everything okay?"

"Jason asked me to stop by his office and drop off Annalise's swim suit. He's taking her for her lesson after work and forgot it. I'll make a quick stop at their house and we'll be on our way."

Although down the block from the Chambers' residence, Lynette and Jason's house was half its size and in need of a paint job. Jason was smart as a whip, but inept as a handyman. Valerie pulled into the driveway. Susan hopped out and made a beeline for Annalise's dresser where she retrieved a pink, ruffled swimsuit. *Lynette had one like this when she was Annalise's age, but Lynette's was blue.* Susan tucked it into her purse on her way back to the car.

Parking on campus was generally a challenge, but they lucked into a vacant metered spot. When they walked into Jason's office, he was consoling a pretty redhead.

"Susan and Valerie, this is Madison Chambers— Harold Chambers' wife. The man who died on the plane. She's a colleague. Madison, this is my mother-in-law and her friend, Valerie."

"I'm sorry about your husband."

Slim and wrinkle-free, Madison Chambers looked more like the daughter than the wife.

"I don't believe it. It's too awful." She was sobbing so hard, Susan could barely make out the words and wondered what she was doing at work. Jason seemed to read her mind.

"Madison is picking up a few things. She won't be back here for a while."

Susan said, "We were with your husband on the plane when he died."

Madison's face turned pale under her tears. "You were? Please, tell me what you know."

"Just that when we landed, I couldn't wake him up. He was…he was dead. I'm so sorry."

Madison Chambers fell into Jason's office chair sobbing. "Someone has to find the man who did this. The detective said he was poisoned."

"The police are on it. We were just at the station."

Jason said, "Madison knows I'm married to the lead detective. The only detective at the moment."

"Did you hear him talking to anyone on the phone while he was on the plane? I know he couldn't when he was in the air, but maybe before or...never mind."

"No, I'm sorry," said Susan.

"It was that parent. The one who owns the nursery. He came by the house the night before Harold left on his trip threatening to sue him for taking bribes from parents."

"What sort of bribes?" asked Susan.

"Bribes to insure their children were accepted into top colleges. Nonsense." His son didn't get into Harvard and he had to blame it on someone."

"Which parent?"

"Carmine Vitulli. His son didn't get into Harvard and he blamed it on Harold. I told the police already."

"Did he have access to the snacks Harold packed?"

"Well, Harold had his bags packed and ready to go by the front door like he always did the night before a trip. Let me think. I went into the kitchen. I heard them arguing. Then Harold got a phone call so he stepped away just for a minute or so."

Valerie said, "He couldn't have opened the little bags, sprinkled cyanide, and tied them back up in a few minutes like that."

"What if he brought tainted snacks with him?" suggested Susan.

Madison said, "They sell those Snacky Sax everywhere since they appeared on *Shark Tank*. And everyone knows Harold had a penchant for sweets."

Jason said, "Thanks for bringing the bathing suit by. I think we need to let Madison collect her things and get home."

"Of course." Susan turned to Madison. "My condolences."

Stepping outside into the bright sunlight, she said to Valerie, "Do you want to take a little side trip?"

"I could use a few shrubs for the new house. Want me to see if there's a nursery around here?"

Chapter 5

Shortly after leaving the university, Valerie said, "I found Carmine's nursery on this app. It's not too far. Turn right at the light."

"I'm on it." Susan said. "Lynette has her hands full with Jackson gone now. It may be a while before she gets out here and if it turns out to be a dead end, we'll have saved her the trouble. We have to be careful not to overstep our boundaries, though." She said it mostly to remind herself since this had been a constant source of conflict between her and Lynette.

"I've heard those words from Jazzy more than once."

"Did she decide to make an offer on the house?"

"She loved it by the photos alone and she checked out the neighborhood. Good schools, and low crime rate. I'm waiting to hear from her."

They passed a sign for Carmine's Nursery. Susan turned onto a shaded dirt road flanked by a barbed wire fence. She stepped on the gas and her Prius reluctantly chugged up the mountain.

Valerie pointed out the window. "Aren't those greenhouses?"

"They are." Susan turned and parked in front of the nursery. They hopped out onto the gravel and entered a small shop full of garden supplies, seeds, and ceramic garden gnomes. Despite a small fan perched on a side table, the humidity gave Susan an instant headache.

An elderly woman wearing a red and white apron smiled at them from behind the register as she finished ringing up a customer. "Can I help you?"

Valerie took the lead. "I'm buying a house and need some shrubbery to put out front. Can you help me?"

"I just run the gift shop, but my son is out back and he's an expert. He'll set you up."

"Where is he?"

"Check the first greenhouse. His name is Carmine. Tall, curly hair...you can't miss him." She whispered, "He's a few decades older than anyone else out there."

Susan grabbed a bag of Snacky Sax from a straw basket beside the register. "Are these any good?"

"People seem to think so. Personally, I'm not fond of nuts. Locally made. Gal who came up with the idea is making a killing since her Shark Tank deal."

Susan read the ingredients. "I'm diabetic and have to watch my sugar but my stomach is rumbling." She inspected the wrapper and, satisfied it came in under the sugar threshold, she tossed it on the counter, counted out exact change from the bottom of her over-sized purse, then followed Valerie outside into the first greenhouse.

She wiped the sweat off her bifocals and spotted Carmine right away spraying the plants with a mister. "Carmine Vitulli?" When she called his name, he jumped, whipped around, and she felt the glorious cold spray on her face.

"I'm so sorry."

"Don't apologize. It's only water." She was reluctant to dry it off, appreciating the coolness.

"What can I do for you?"

Valerie said, "I'm looking for shrubbery that can hold up under an Eastern exposure. My daughter and I are about to purchase a home."

"Congratulations." He set down the mister. "Follow me. I've got several great choices."

Susan noticed the bags of fertilizer both inside the greenhouse and in the wheelbarrows on the way to the shrubbery section and wondered if they contained cyanide. She made a mental note of the brand name stamped on the bags.

Carmine pointed to a shrub. "These do well in the sun and hold up to the cold winters as well. They don't require a lot of maintenance, just a little pruning a few times a year."

A young man with the same slender build and curly hair approached and smiled at them. "Dad, a lady wants to know how many rose bushes she needs for a six by six space. I wasn't sure."

"Tell her I'll be with her in a minute."

When he walked off, Susan said, "That's your son? What a handsome young man." She had noticed the garden gloves. "In line to inherit the business one day?"

"Oh, no. My son's going to be a surgeon. He's taking the year to work and raise money for tuition."

"So he's smart and handsome."

"And athletic."

"I think they call that a triple threat," said Susan.

"He should be going to Harvard. Their loss. He's nationally ranked and had a 6.0 GPA to boot, but don't get me started."

Susan's pulse quickened at the fortuitous opening. "I'll bet the slot went to some actor's kid or some big donor's kid. Not fair. My son just graduated medical school but he had to work his way through on his own merit and owes a mortgage worth of student loans."

"Tell me about it. Worked triple time to send him to a college prep program. The owner guaranteed he'd guide him to an acceptance letter." Carmine kicked the hose.

"But he didn't, right? Same thing happened to one of my son's friends. And it was supposed to be a money back guarantee. Good luck with that. He looked into a lawsuit but forget it."

"Too expensive, right? I looked into it myself. Damn thing is, I paid the tuition. Still, it went to the highest bidder if you know what I mean. Deep pockets. Bribes under the table."

"So unfair. I saw on the news they caught a couple of celebrities getting their kids into Ivy League schools like that."

Valerie said, "And they'll never see prison time. Just watch. I'd kill the bastard if I were in your shoes."

Susan noticed the veins popping out of Carmine's neck. "Damn right. Someone should."

The man's son came back. "Dad, she's in a hurry."

"Okay, I'm coming." He turned to Valerie. "Can I put together an estimate? I'll need the dimensions."

"I'll get back to you after the sale is finalized. I grabbed a card from the counter in the gift shop."

"Okay then. Looking forward to doing business with you."

When they got back to the car, Valerie said, "We have to check the ingredients in that fertilizer. I've got the brand name."

Susan said, "Me, too. And he has motive and opportunity. Madison said he stopped by the house the night Harold left for St. Louis."

"Thing is, he doesn't strike me as a killer. He was so helpful and he didn't try to sell us the most expensive shrubs. I paid attention to the price tags."

"You never can tell. Ted Bundy's neighbors said what a good guy he was. Besides having access to fertilizer, we know he sells Snacky Sax in the gift shop. He could have poisoned it beforehand and switched it out or taken the poison with him to Chambers' house."

"That's premeditation. You think he planned this?" asked Valerie.

"He told us a law suit was too expensive, yet that's exactly what he threatened to do. Could have been a ruse to get in the door. Let's get home."

On the way home, Jazmin called.

"Mom, I got the mortgage all set and I turned in an offer. I'll let you know when I hear back from the sellers."

"You work fast. Did you show Elijah the pictures of the back yard with the swing set?"

"Oh, yeah. He's ready to move in tomorrow. Even suggested there was room to put in a pool."

"We can look into one of those above the ground ones. Susan's granddaughter takes swimming lessons here. I'll get the information."

"Mom, don't get ahead of us. We don't even know if the offer will be accepted and it has to pass inspection. Besides, with the down payment and moving expenses, it'll be a while before we can afford a pool."

"I think you'll like Westbrook. Lynette sure has her hands full. She can't wait for you to get here."

"And I've got *my* hands full wrapping things up here. Do you know how expensive moving companies are? And the mountain of toys in Elijah's room to go through? Gotta go. I'll call when I hear about the house."

When they got home, Susan pulled out her laptop. Valerie did the same.

"I'll look up the fertilizer; why don't you check out Harvard's requirements and acceptance rates. Maybe look at the track team stats as well."

"I'm on it. I'm going to see if I can check the son's record to verify what Carmine told us about him being a top student is true."

"I don't know how you're going to get those records."

"You're the retired teacher. If I can't, I'll bet you can. Don't you have school connections?"

"My father is dating Janet, the librarian at the high school. Hmmm."

"For now, check the fertilizer."

Susan searched and found the ingredients. *Now to find out how much it takes to kill someone and how to extract the cyanide from the fertilizer.*

She searched for over an hour. "I can't find anything about extracting cyanide out of fertilizer."

"It's not information that should be easy to find. Maybe you need to go to the dark web."

"Do you know how to access the dark web?"

"No idea."

"How are you doing with the Harvard stats?"

"Tons of valedictorians are turned away every year so even having a 6.0 GPA isn't a guarantee of getting in. They also look at SAT scores. We don't know how the boys did on those."

"But how about the kid the officer told us about? Sean White, right? The one with the lower GPA. Did they accept anyone at that level?"

"Not according to this curve. It says something about athletic and talent exceptions."

"So maybe this kid was an athlete. Carmine made his threat at a track meet."

"Maybe. Why don't we talk to your father's girlfriend at the high school? Maybe she knows all of them and can tell us more."

"They're on summer session, but the library is open limited hours. At least it used to be." She Googled the hours. "If we hurry, we can make it before they close."

They gathered their things and went to the school. Janet was busy taking inventory but when she saw them, she smiled.

"Susan? What a nice surprise."

She gave her a kiss on the cheek. "This is my friend, Valerie, from St. Louis."

"The one whose daughter is going to be Lynette's partner, right?"

"Yes. She thinks she found a house already. Anyhow, we wanted to ask if you can tell us about a boy with the last name Vitulli."

"Bruno Vitulli. Nice boy but rather high strung. He was always in here hitting the books."

"We heard he was turned down by Harvard but some other classmate with lesser credentials got in." said Susan.

"Ah, that story has legs. Sean White. Struggled to make B's and I hardly ever saw him in here studying. Daddy's rich and got him enrolled at Succex. Next thing you know, he's got a choice of Ivy League schools while Bruno and his friend Tyler are out in the cold."

"Maybe they didn't do well on the SATS?" Valerie ran her fingers along the book spines.

"Oh, wrong. They both got nearly perfect scores. Both were National Merit Scholars and scholar-athletes."

"What about Sean White? Was he an athlete or did he have some special talent that may have gotten him an advantage?" said Susan.

"Not that I know of. He got in because his daddy enrolled him in Succex. And he made the highest bid."

"Bribed the colleges?"

"Bribed Harold Chambers to get his son accepted. I don't think the colleges knew he was doctoring the applications, but maybe that's just me being naïve."

Valerie said, "I heard Bruno's father threatened to kill Chambers right in the middle of a track meet."

"Dad's got a quick temper, just like his son. But he's a good man. He runs a nursery. Helped me get my garden started. He was counting on a scholarship. Harvard offers free tuition these days if you meet the financial criteria. Now Bruno has to work a year just to help pay tuition at SUNY Westbrook."

Valerie checked out the Dewy decimal numbers on the ends of the rows.

Janet said, "What are you looking for?"

"Are there books that tell you how to extract cyanide from fertilizer?"

Janet rubbed her ear. "I'm sorry but I'm not sure I heard you correctly. Extracting cyanide from fertilizer?"

Susan said, "It's a hunch we had. We sat with Harold Chambers on the plane and saw signs he may have been poisoned."

"And Carmine Vitulli owns a nursery. I see where you're going with this. If anyone knows how to do something like that it'd be his son, Bruno. Bruno is a chemistry whiz. Won the state science competition last year. Extract it? He probably knows how to make it."

"Thanks, Janet. You may be on to something."

Chapter 6

Mike plopped his lunchbox on the kitchen counter. "How'd it go at the station?"

Susan stirred a pot of chicken chili with a wooden spoon. "We told Lynette what we saw. She's swamped with Jackson gone."

"She's going to be more swamped, now."

"What do you mean?"

"Didn't you hear it on the news? While I was at work, the bank across the street from the permit's office was robbed. We watched the police surround the place, but the robbers escaped. I'm sure the police department is under pressure to solve this with armed robbers on the loose."

"Then Valerie and I have all the more reason to take up some of the slack and help figure out who killed Harold Chambers."

"Has it even been deemed a murder?"

"The way Lynette was questioning us? Yes."

Valerie's phone buzzed and she walked into the living room. Minutes later, she screamed. Mike and Susan ran in.

Susan's heart pounded. "What's wrong? Are you okay?"

Valerie tucked the phone into her pocket and gave them high fives. "The sellers accepted Jazmin's offer and are fast tracking the closing. Looks like we've got ourselves a house."

Susan hugged her. "You know you almost gave me a heart attack. That's fantastic. You'll need some things for the new place."

"I noticed signs for an outlet mall. We'll need some window treatments, maybe some lamps."

"They've got great deals on towels and linens."

Valerie said, "And a broom. You're not supposed to bring an old broom into a new house. It's bad luck."

"What about a nice welcome mat for the front door?"

"Great idea. I'll put it out before Jazzy sees the place. Elijah is going to love the stars on his bedroom ceiling. I'm going to see if I can find a comforter set with planets and rocket ships on it."

Mike said, "Congratulations. Welcome to Westbrook. I smell chili. Anyone hungry?"

"Absolutely. I'd say we worked up an appetite. It's been a full day." Susan put out straw placemats and turned off the stove. "Valerie made us cornbread."

"It's from a mix, but you can't have chili without corn bread."

"Mike, get the salad from the fridge."

They sat down and started eating.

"So Mike, Susan says you're thinking of retiring."

"I've thought of it on and off since the first heart attack. I've already cut back my hours. I think I'd go crazy being at home all day." He glanced at Susan.

"You'd find plenty to do, and I've got my own life so don't think I'd be getting in your way."

"I didn't mean that. Not really. It's just, look at how bored you were when you first retired."

"But I found my groove and you will too."

"We'll see. I've been feeling good and it's not like we can't use the paycheck."

Valerie said, "This chili is delicious. You'd never know it's made with pureed beets."

Mike made a face and gulped his water. "Beets? Yuck." He pushed his plate away.

Susan said, "You didn't know the difference until Valerie told you." Her phone buzzed.

"I don't know this number."

"Then don't answer it," said Mike."

She picked it up. "Hello? Madison Chambers? Of course I remember meeting you."

Mike gave her a quizzical look.

"You want us to meet tomorrow?"

"I found something I think is important," the voice said. "I tried to get a hold of your daughter, but she's all wrapped up in the bank robbery that happened today and frankly, I'm not sure she believes there was any foul play involved in my husband's murder. I got your number from Jason. He's bragged about your sleuthing ability in the past."

"He has? I'm flattered." The peacock in her fanned her feathers.

"Can you come by tomorrow morning? I'll text you the address."

"Sure."

She put the phone back on the table.

Mike said, "I thought you and Valerie were going shopping tomorrow?"

"We are. After we talk to Madison."

"You don't find it strange?"

"Her asking for my help?"

"Jason recommending you. He knows how irritated Lynette gets when you interfere."

"He's a smart man. He sees my value. Aren't you at least going to eat your salad?"

"What did you slip into it? Are those mushrooms, or some sort of tofu concoction?"

"You're impossible."

Valerie said, "The two of you really make me miss my Charlie."

Susan and Mike answered in unison, "You miss this?"

Valerie wiped a tear from her eye. "Appreciate what you have." She took a tissue from her pocket. "By the way, I think Susan and I will stop at the nursery tomorrow and see if we can get some landscaping going before Jazzy and Elijah get here."

Mike made himself a ham sandwich while Susan and Valerie finished the chili. After dinner, they played a game of Scrabble and turned in early.

The next morning, Susan and Valerie headed to Madison's, stopping at the bakery for muffins. A dozen for Madison—one for each of them to eat on the way. The Chambers lived around the corner from the university in the yellow estate the realtor had pointed out. Susan wondered if they had any children or, for that matter, grandchildren. Madison was way too young to be a grandmother but if it were a second marriage…She parked in the driveway. Valerie hopped out and started walking.

"Susan, are you coming?"

"Yes." By the time she wiped her sticky hands with a tissue and threw it back into her purse, Valerie had knocked on the front door. Susan caught up to her.

Madison, even without makeup, looked elegant in yoga pants and a long t-shirt. "Susan, right? Can I call you that?"

"Of course. And you met Valerie at Jason's office. What can we help you with?" She handed the bakery box to Madison, then they followed her into the living room. Danish furniture. Certainly didn't seem like something her husband would have been comfortable sitting in. She remembered how he barely fit in the airplane seat.

"The night before Harold went to St. Louis, I told you about the angry father who came by. I forgot to tell you about the young man I saw hiding behind the bushes."

"Hiding? While Carmine Vitulli was here?"

"He was wearing a hoodie even in this heat. When Vitulli stormed out, I ran to make sure the kitchen door was locked and I saw him in the back yard. With all that happened, I'd nearly forgotten."

"Did he take anything?"

"No. I think he knew I spotted him when I went to lower the blinds. He took off through the neighbor's yard."

"Was it locked?" said Valerie. "You said you went to check the kitchen door."

Madison's pale face turned the color of her hair. "No. I'd forgotten to lock it when I came in from the garden earlier."

"So it's possible he snuck in earlier?"

"Well, after I worked in the garden, I went to take a shower, and Harold was upstairs packing. I suppose it's possible."

Susan chimed in. "Do you remember anything about his appearance? Tall, short?"

Valerie sat forward. "Did you see the color of his skin?"

"He wore jeans and the hoodie was bunched up around his face. And it was dark. He was slender and I guess medium height."

"Show us where he was," said Valerie. They followed her to the yard. It had been nearly a week, but attempting to be proactive, Susan looked for footprints.

Valerie wandered out to the garden and found broken tomato plants near the wooden fence separating the yard from the neighbor's yard.

"Were these plants broken when you were out in the garden earlier?"

Madison bent down and ran her hand over the plants. "No, they weren't."

Valerie pointed. "If he ran through the garden and hopped this fence, he had to be in good shape. It's as high as my chin."

Susan, who was slightly taller, inspected the fence all the way around. Near the garden, she saw a dark stain against the unpainted wood. "Could this be blood?"

Madison looked. "Could be. Harold hadn't gotten around to sanding the fence yet. We replaced it last summer."

Valerie said, "He may have scraped his hand. With jeans and a hoodie, the rest of his body would have been protected."

"Maybe the police can identify him by sending the blood to a lab," said Madison.

Susan doubted the small amount, even if it was blood, would be helpful, but didn't want to disappoint Madison. "You should call my daughter and tell her. Maybe she can send someone to interview the neighbors. The neighbor on the other side of this fence, for example, might have caught a glimpse."

"I'll do that."

In the car, Valerie said, "We know of at least two teenage boys who had a motive to kill Harold."

"What makes you say it was a teenager?"

"Hoodie, slender…successfully hopping a fence and running fast enough to get away?"

"Bruno Vitulli, or Tyler McGinnis, the officer's son. They both run track and both got cheated out of their number one school."

"And poor Bruno has to take a year off and work in his father's nursery just to get tuition together for a state school."

Susan started the car. "After the mall, I have an idea."

"Me, too. Now that I'm about to be a homeowner, perhaps a trip to the nursery is in order."

Chapter 7

When they pulled up to Carmine's nursery, a large delivery truck blocked the small parking area. Carmine ran out of the gift shop and waved to them.

"Come, you can park around the side." He ran ahead and directed them down a dirt road. "Anywhere along here is fine."

Susan pulled in next to a storage shed, under a flowering tree. *Too bad Mike just washed the car.*

Carmine wiped his brow with his bandana. "Back so soon? Does that mean you bought the house?"

"We sure did. My daughter and grandson haven't seen it yet. I was hoping to have the shrubbery put in by the time they come."

"Eastern exposure, right?"

Valerie said, "You've got a good memory." They followed him around the hot house and into the back area. They passed Bruno pushing a wheelbarrow with his gloved hands.

"Did you figure out the dimensions?"

It was difficult to hear over the rumble of an engine. "What did you say? What's that noise?"

"The delivery truck is leaving. I asked if you had the dimensions."

"Oh, no. That was dumb. Came all the way out here and didn't measure first."

"It's okay. You can decide what you want, then call me and we'll figure out numbers."

"I've always lived in the city." Valerie stopped shouting now that the truck was gone and it was quiet. "Is there any way I can have the shrubs installed?"

"You mean planted? Yes, our fees are reasonable. We'll set something up."

Carmine's phone rang. "A police detective? Here? Sure. I'll be right there." He turned to Valerie, "Excuse me but I need to take care of something. You've got my card, right?"

"Sure do." When he was out of earshot, Valerie whispered, "Do you think it's about the murder? Do you think Lynette is here?"

"If she sees us, we are here to buy shrubs, like we said. But first, let's try to get a peek at Bruno's hands. Follow me." Susan led her toward the apple orchard. "There's Bruno. Don't you want to ask him something?"

Following her lead, Valerie approached Bruno and said, "Excuse me. I forgot to ask your father if you do actual landscaping?"

When he turned around, she spotted the ear pods, waited for him to remove them, and repeated herself.

"Yeah. Dad's the planner, I do the hard labor."

Susan looked at the gloves. Then she fumbled in her purse. She opened her wallet and spilled coins on the ground. "Oh, my goodness. I was looking for the cloth to clean my glasses and I'm such a klutz."

Valerie started to bend down, but Susan nudged her while Bruno's head was turned.

Bruno said, "I'll get it." He bent down to gather the coins that he wasn't able to grasp—until he pulled off his glove. His hand was swaddled in gauze.

"Thank you. Not so easy to bend down when you get to be my age."

Valerie said, "What happened to your hand?"

Bruno put his good hand over the one with the bandage as if to hide it. "I scraped it on a rose bush. Should have known roses have thorns." He forced a chuckle while he put the gloves back on. "I gotta get back to work. We'll be closing soon and I've got to lock up the equipment." He stuck the earbuds back in his ears and clicked something on his watch. Faint music bled through the earbuds.

It was nearing dinner time, but with the long summer days, Susan thought it was earlier. They had spent more time than she'd realized at the mall comparing throw pillows and space-themed comforter sets. Bruno entered the glass hothouse and Susan motioned for Valerie to follow.

Susan's glasses steamed up the minute she stepped inside the hothouse. Orchids and delicate flowering plants filled the space. Bruno took the earbuds out of his ears and turned around. "I thought you'd left. Do you need something else?"

Valerie said, "We wanted to ask a few questions."

"I'll write down the directions for watering and fertilizing your new shrubs and you can always call if you get confused."

Valerie winced at the word confused. People see an elderly woman and think Alzheimer's. It wasn't the first time. "It's not about the shrubs. It's about Harold Chambers, the owner of Succex. You know he," she cleared her throat, "died recently."

"So I heard. I don't know how I can be of help."

"He was seated between my friend and me on the plane where he died. His widow asked for our help since we were the last to see him alive. Poor thing is a mess."

"And?"

"Didn't you attend that program he ran? Succex?"

"Waste of money. No one told my Dad he had to scrape together bribe money on top of tuition."

"Are you saying the kids that enrolled in Succex and got accepted at their dream schools bought their way in?"

"Their parents bought their way in. Excuse me, it wasn't bribery. It was *contributions to Chamber's educational scholarship foundation*. Kids much less qualified than me got into Ivy Leagues for a price."

Susan said, "I'd have been furious if I was your father. Or you, for that matter."

Valerie said, "Harold Chambers got what was coming to him. Died of cyanide poisoning. Ain't that weird? They think it came from a Snacky Sax treat he was eating on the plane."

"How would cyanide get in there? Snacky Sax is a locally manufactured product. I haven't heard of any recalls."

"We think it was done deliberately. Someone targeted Harold Chambers." She studied his face for a reaction.

"That's sick."

Valerie said, "Someone had to have access to cyanide. And to Harold Chamber's carry-on bag. Cyanide's an ingredient in fertilizer, right?"

Susan added, "And my friend who's your school librarian told me you're quite the chemistry whiz."

Bruno let go of the hose he was holding and put his hands on his hips. "You have to be kidding. What are you implying? That I killed him?"

"We know someone snuck around in the Chambers' yard the night before Harold Chambers left for a conference in St. Louis." Susan wiped off her glasses so she could see his reaction more clearly.

"Someone in shape enough to hop a wooden fence." Valerie circled around him.

"But in his hurry, he scraped his hand and left blood on the fence."

Bruno covered his hand. "This is absurd."

"If you didn't do it, maybe you can tell us about your friend, Tyler McGinnis. He was in the same situation you were, right?"

"Tyler never went to Succex. Besides, Harvard wasn't Tyler's idea, it was his father's. Tyler was offered an athletic scholarship at his first choice— Michigan State. Had he gotten into Harvard, he was braced for a big fight with his dad."

"But you really wanted Harvard, didn't you?" Susan put a sympathetic hand on his shoulder.

Bruno shook her off, grabbed the wheel barrow and shoved it at them, knocking Susan to the ground. She heard the key turn in the door, the glass rattling as he ran out.

Susan stumbled to her feet and picked up her glasses from the ground. Valerie was already at the door yanking on the handle.

Valerie pounded on the glass. "Come back here!" When Bruno was clearly out of sight, she switched to, "Help, we're locked in." She dug in her heels and pulled on the door handle with all her weight behind her. "Let us out!"

Susan foraged through her purse for her phone, then dialed the nursery number. "I'm not getting a signal."

Valerie tried her phone. "Me, neither. It's barely after six. Do you think Carmine's gone already? And wouldn't Lynette have noticed your car out front?"

"No, remember? The truck was there and we pulled around the side. She wouldn't have seen it."

"Mike will be looking for you, right?"

"He should be home by now. Maybe he thinks we got hung up at the mall. The mall doesn't close until nine."

"We're literally in a glass house. See any stones? Or rocks? Or sharp tools we can use to break the glass?" Valerie searched the aisles.

Susan picked up a small trowel and hit it against the glass until her arm tired and her shoulder ached. Then she tried to pick up a heavy clay pot. "Help me. Maybe this will work."

Valerie pushed a table of plants to the side, giving them a clear shot at the glass. Then she and Susan each grabbed an end. "On three. One, two...give it all you've got...three."

The pot didn't even crack, let alone make a dent, in the glass. Out of breath, they both collapsed onto the dirt floor.

Valerie said, "How about digging our way underneath?"

Susan picked up the trowel "Like with this? Seriously?"

"You have a better idea?"

The sky grew darker as the sun sank behind the mountains. Susan tried her phone again. "Still no signal."

"At worst, someone will find us in the morning, right?"

"I don't want to spend the night here. My clothes are soaked in sweat already and I'm starving."

"Me, too. Too bad we didn't bring along some Snacky Sax."

"Not funny. Well, maybe a little funny."

"Let's put our heads together and think this through so we can get out of here."

Chapter 8

Mike paced back and forth across the kitchen with the phone to his ear. "Lynette, your mom and Valerie haven't come home. They should have been here hours ago. The mall is closed by now, right?"

"Did you try calling her?"

"Of course. It goes to voicemail."

"Did you try Valerie?"

"Same thing."

"I'm coming over."

Mike checked the kitchen calendar in case he'd forgotten an appointment she'd mentioned. Nothing. Ludwig meowed from the food bowl. Susan never let it get empty, but every morsel was gone. She must not have come back to the house. "Hungry? I'm not going to let you starve." When Johann heard the cat food hit the bowl, he darted off the back of the sofa, into the kitchen.

Lynette knocked, then used her key before Mike could reach the front door. Lynette had a knack for staying calm in most situations, but agitation crept into her voice. "Did they come back?" Mike shook his head. "Did she mention anywhere else they may have been going?"

"Valerie's house deal went through. Maybe they stopped there to have a look around."

"They haven't closed. They wouldn't have the keys yet."

"Even if they took in a movie or stopped at the grocery store, they'd be home by now."

"I'll try Jonathan." Lynette took out her phone. "Jonathan, have you heard from my mom today?"

"No, why? She'd mentioned us getting together for dinner one night but nothing concrete. Wait a second. Janet wants to talk to you."

"Lynette? I saw your mom and Valerie earlier today. They came by the school library."

"The library? What did they want?"

"She was asking about some of our students."

"Which students?"

"Tyler McGinnis and Bruno Vitulli. I told her they were both smart as a whip. National Merit Scholars in fact. Then she asked about Sean White. He wasn't a top notch student but was accepted at Harvard."

The veins in Lynette's neck popped out. "Anything else?"

"Something about making cyanide out of fertilizer. Wanted to know if we had any books on it. I told her I didn't think so."

"Did she say where they were going after they left the library?"

"No. Sorry."

"You've been a big help. Tell Jonathan I'll call when we find them."

Mike said, "Well?"

"Where's Mom's laptop?"

"On the sofa, why?"

Lynette sat down on the sofa and opened it. Susan hadn't bothered to log out and it was easy to access her history. "Dad, look. She was googling how to make cyanide out of fertilizer. She's meddling in an investigation again."

"She said something about visiting Madison Chambers this morning."

"Madison Chambers. I'll try her."

Lynette found her number. "Mrs. Chambers? This is Detective Greene."

"Did you find my husband's killer yet?"

"Not yet. Did you have any visitors this morning? An overweight black woman and a chunky white lady with glasses? In their sixties? The white one is my mother."

"Susan and Valerie. I asked them to come by. I remembered something and had tried all day to get in touch with you but I got voicemail. I even tried the number for the front desk and they said you were busy."

"We were dealing with a major situation yesterday. Still are, in fact."

"Well, that's why I called your mother. She and her friend were perfectly willing to help."

"What information did you give her that you wanted to tell me?"

"I remembered seeing someone in a hoodie outside in my back yard the night before Harold left. I realized I hadn't locked the kitchen door and it's possible this person snuck in and swapped the Snacky Sax."

"What did the intruder look like?"

"Medium height, thin. Ran fast and hopped the fence into my neighbor's yard. You should check with my neighbors, you know. They might have seen him."

"We will definitely follow up. I'll keep you posted as the investigation unfolds." She shook her head and stuck the phone back in her pocket. "Dad, let's go. I think I know where they are."

*****

Valerie checked every inch of the hothouse searching for a way out while intermittently trying her phone in hopes of getting a signal. Susan sat quietly on the ground.

"Susan, are you okay? I know it's hot as blazin' in here, but you don't look right."

"My head feels like it's going to float away and I'm very tired."

"You're probably hungry." Valerie dug through her purse. "Nothing. Usually I can find a little something but since we've been trying to eat healthier, I don't tempt myself. You're shaking."

"It's my blood sugar. With my diabetes, I can't go long stretches without eating."

"Don't you carry glucose pills or somethin'?"

"No. I can't remember the last time I went more than a few hours without eating." She felt hot, then cold. Her eyes were like iron curtains.

"Susan, stay awake. What happens if this gets worse?"

"Huh? I could pass out or slip into a coma." She closed her eyes and curled into a ball on the floor like she'd seen her cats do many times.

Valerie tried her phone again. No signal. Good for nothing except the flashlight app. She walked to every corner of the hot house holding the phone up as high as she could.

"I've got this, hang in there." She noticed some of the plants were being held to a wooden stake by wire. She extricated one of the wires and stuck it into the lock. It broke in her hand.

"Susan?" She shook her and shouted at her. "Wake up. Help will be here soon." She hoped, but knew they'd most likely be in there all night. She didn't know a lot about diabetes, but this wasn't looking good. She couldn't wake her friend.

"I'm going to try using a credit card. Hang in there." She grabbed a card from her wallet and tried to slip it between the lock and the door frame. She tried a second card, then a third, hoping they came in different thicknesses, though she knew better. She spotted the hose.

"Susan, can you wake up? How about some water." She gently shook her. "Susan?"

Valerie remembered the sugar packet she tucked in her purse at the airport. "Susan, here. Eat this." Susan didn't move, and Valerie knew better than to try to feed someone who was unconscious. Valerie turned on the water, took off her sock, got it damp and placed it on Susan's forehead. "You have to wake up. I don't want you to die."

*****

Lynette sped through town and up the mountain road, Mike in the passenger seat. She made a sharp turn into the parking area, slammed on the brakes, and turned off the car. She reached over Mike, grabbed a flashlight from the glove compartment, and jumped out onto the gravel.

"Come on Dad. I'll bet they're here somewhere." She jogged around the side of the building. "I see Mom's car!" She ran to it and looked inside. "Mom? Valerie?"

Mike, panting, had caught up to her. "Did you find them?"

"They aren't in there. And there are bags from the mall in the back seat."

She ran to the door of the gift shop and tugged the handle. "It's locked. Let's look around the grounds."

Mike followed her along the orchard and around to the greenhouses. "I don't see anyone in there, but it's so dark, I may be wrong."

"Wait. I see a little light from that one."

"Where?"

"Near the ground by the door. Come on." They flew to the hothouse and yanked on the door. Valerie jumped up. "We're locked in. Help. Your mom's not well."

Lynette picked up a hoe that was lying on the ground. "Stand back." She smashed the glass, reached in, and opened the lock.

"Mom? Wake up." She shook her gently at first, then with more force.

"She said it's her blood sugar."

"Call 911."

"There's no signal in here."

"Dad, help me get her up." They pulled her up and carried her to Lynette's car where she used the radio to call for help. "Mom. Come on, now. Dad, go in the trunk and get out the first aid kit."

Valerie said, "Wait. I know this is crazy but I have a packet of sugar in my pocket from when I got coffee at work." She tried handing it to Lynette.

"No, I've got emergency Glucagon in the first aid kit. That will bring up her blood sugar right away."

Mike returned with the first aid kit. Lynette took out the Glucagon and stabbed Susan in the thigh with the needle.

Valerie said, "Susan, come back to us, We're safe now."

Susan stirred and rubbed her head. "Where am I? My head hurts."

Lynette opened the glove compartment and took out a small package of Ritz Bits peanut butter crackers. "Eat these. Annalise won't mind sharing her snack. You have to keep up your blood sugar."

Susan took one from the small foil bag. "I remember being stuck in the hot house and feeling faint. What happened?"

Valerie said, "I'll fill you in later."

A siren whirred, screaming louder as it approached. The paramedics hopped out and loaded Susan onto a stretcher.

"I'm okay now, I just needed food."

"Mom, it's either go to the hospital, or get in the car and explain what you were doing here."

Susan put her head back down on the stretcher. "I may need a doctor after all."

Chapter 9

Susan and Valerie spent the next morning relaxing.
After lunch, they baked an apple pie to bring to
Lynette's, then watched a little TV while waiting for
Mike to get home.

Mike gave her a kiss, then set his lunch box on the
counter while Valerie took a call from Jazmin out on
the back porch.

"Hey, let me change and we can be on our way. Did
you and Valerie pick up dessert?"

"Pick up? We baked a pie."

"And wasn't it more fun than chasing a potential
killer into a hot house, getting locked in, and almost
dying from low blood sugar?"

She gave him a playful swat. Valerie came inside
and stuck her phone into her purse. "Jazzy says the
inspection is set for tomorrow and if all goes well, the
closing is Friday. She and Elijah are coming out for the
weekend. They'll arrive tomorrow evening. She said
they'd take an Uber to the hotel."

"Nonsense. We can pick them up. If we hadn't
turned Lynette's room into a home office, and Evan's
into extra storage, they could have stayed with us."

"Elijah's excited. The hotel has an indoor pool and
he loves those breakfast buffets. Can you drop me off at
the new place tomorrow afternoon?"

"Drop you off? I want to follow the inspector around
and make sure he doesn't miss anything."

Mike came down stairs. "Let's go."

Lynette and Jason lived in a quiet development near the university and around the corner from where Madison and Harold Chambers lived, but it might as well have been a different city.

The Chambers lived off the main street leading into the university in a huge, two story house behind a barrier of field stones, weeping willows, and a wrap-around porch as wide as Susan's kitchen. Lynette and Jason's place was a modest three-bedroom, with a driveway in need of repaving and a front door in need of repainting.

Valerie carried the pie, leaving Susan's hands free to pick up Annalise when the door opened.

"You're getting heavy. I can't believe you're going to be in kindergarten."

"You can put me down."

"Not on your life." She kissed her tummy like she'd done since Annalise was little and elicited the same exquisite giggle. Mike scooped up Mia, who was just getting through an extended stranger anxiety phase and unexpectedly smiled at Valerie rather than hiding her face in the crook of her grandpa's shoulder.

Valerie handed the pie to Lynette. "Your mom and I made this."

"Smells delicious. Congratulations. I can't wait to see your new place and to have Jazmin here. We are so overwhelmed at the station."

Jonathan and Janet sipped red wine in the living room. Jonathan stood up and gave Susan a hug.

Susan said, "Where's Jason?"

"He's outside grilling steaks and corn on the cob. He mentioned eating outside but it's so muggy, I thought we'd be more comfortable in the dining room. You feeling better, Mom?"

"Much."

"Good. After dinner we'll have a little talk about staying out of police business. Again."

"We weren't interfering. It's not like I messed up a crime scene or anything."

"Not this time. You'd been doing so much better and then you go and put your life and your friend's life in danger."

"Hardly. Bruno's just a kid. He got scared, that's all."

"You should have pressed charges, like I recommended."

"Well, he may have bigger trouble to answer to. Madison Chambers saw someone in her backyard the night before Harold's trip."

"I know. I talked to Madison, as well as her neighbor. Then I checked security footage from the neighbor's camera. It was Bruno. He admitted it. But he never went inside the house. The security footage shows him taking off on foot."

Susan said, "You had a busy day. Why was he in the backyard, then?"

"He was worried his father might do something stupid. He followed him there. After his father left, he hopped the fence and went home."

Jason called from the kitchen. "Steaks are done. Come and get them while they're hot."

They filed into the dining room. The aroma of freshly grilled steak had Susan salivating. Although Mike was allowed a little beef now and then according to his heart-healthy guidelines, she tended to stick with baked chicken and had been trying more vegetarian recipes lately. She hadn't eaten steak in ages.

Valerie said, "I'll take some of that corn. Nothing like grilled corn."

Lynette sliced the kernels off the ears for the girls and cut up the two hot dogs Jason grilled for them.

Janet said, "I thought about Bruno and Tyler after you left the other day. Did you hear about those celebrities who were charged with paying off admissions officers to get their kids into college? One got her daughter a swimming scholarship and the kid didn't even know how to swim!"

Valerie said, "In California, right? Like how they photo shopped the kid into the team picture? Money will buy you most anything these days."

Mike said, "I'm surprised a coach would go along with that."

Jason said, "I wouldn't put it past our coach. Madison's office is next door to mine and not too long ago when Harold came by to take her out to lunch, Harold waited in the hall while she finished up a meeting. I heard him on the phone out there saying something about making room on the team and then he laughed. I hadn't thought about it until you mentioned this."

"You think he was talking to the coach?" said Lynette. "It could have been any coach."

"I heard him say "Go Warriors," and then he said, "Good luck tonight." There was a game that night. I watched it."

Susan said, "Hmm."

Lynette grimaced at her. "We'll look into it."

Janet broke the tension. "Any more news on Evan and Cara's wedding?"

"They're both so busy with their residencies they were looking into destination weddings. I offered to do the wedding planning for them, but they didn't take me up on it."

"Good for them," said Lynette. "You'd have gone crazy over the top and out of budget. I had to tame you when I was planning my own wedding or we'd have spent a million dollars we didn't have."

Susan pouted.

"But Mom, I love your enthusiasm. And I know you just wanted things to be perfect—and they were."

"I'd do anything for my kids." She looked at Mia and Annalise. "And for my granddaughters."

Mike said, "Even pay off an admissions counselor to get them into Harvard?"

"If I had to. But they're both so brilliant, they'll do it on their own."

Lynette brought out the pie. "Dessert, anyone?"

Annalise said, "Apple pie? Apples grow on trees in orchards."

"Yes, they do. Then they are picked and sold to stores and people like Grandma and Miss Valerie can turn them into pies." She stopped.

"Mom what's wrong?"

"Apple orchards. Carmine's nursery has an apple orchard. Didn't I read something about making poison from apple cores somewhere? Maybe I read it in a book…"

Jason cleared his throat. "Coffee anyone?"

Chapter 10

The next day, Susan assimilated the information she'd looked up after they'd gotten back from Lynette's. She was right. Cyanide could be made by crushing apple seeds. It'd take a lot of seeds, but Carmine owned an orchard for heaven's sake. Bruno suspected his father might do something dangerous and followed him to the Chambers' house the night before Harold left. Was he right?

Valerie plopped down on the sofa with her laptop. "Look what I found out about the coach."

"How did you find out who he is?"

"Please. A quick click on the university website took care of that. I looked at his bio. He's been at three different universities in the past ten years. Doesn't that seem like a lot?"

"Where was he before? He could have been climbing the ladder."

"He was at Duke. They have a good basketball team, don't they?"

"I'd have to ask Mike, but Duke is a big deal. Strange that he'd leave."

"What if he was fired?"

"I doubt SUNY Westbrook would have picked him up in that case."

"How about we check out Succex? Is it far from here?"

"No, just downtown and off the main street. We can go to lunch afterwards."

"Don't forget the inspection is later today. Let me make myself presentable and we can go."

Half an hour later, they stood in front of Succex. The building looked like it could have once been a legal or medical office—brick with green shutters and trim, neatly manicured shrubs on either side of the door, and a mat in front that read, "Succex doesn't happen by chance."

A secretary attired neatly in a cotton dress smiled at them from behind her desk. "Can I help you?"

The air was refrigerator cold, which Susan appreciated. She noticed an office with Harold Chambers' name on it and a makeshift memorial with flowers and stuffed animals outside the door. "Was that the office of the man who died recently?"

"Yes. The students placed those there. Mr. Chambers is greatly missed. His clients looked up to him like a second father."

Susan thought that was a little weird. A mentor or a guide she could see, but a father?

"There aren't many students here," said Susan.

"Well, it is the middle of summer. Wait until a month from now when the kids and their parents start panicking about early admission deadlines."

Valerie glanced at the "Wall of Succex"—an oversized bulletin board with pictures of young men and women and the schools where they were accepted. She wandered over and read the captions.

"Yale, Cal Tech, Brown—impressive," said Valerie.

"There are more but we'd need a bigger board. We're hoping things will continue running smoothly once Mr. Chambers' partner takes over."

"Partner? Who is it?" asked Susan.

"Top secret. He's been a silent partner since the school opened. Mr. Chambers said he didn't like the limelight. Bit of a hermit I imagine."

"Then isn't it going to be uncomfortable for him to step forward?"

"Honestly, speculation is that he's going to either sell the business or hire a manager for the day to day operations."

"And no one has any idea who it is?"

"Nope."

Susan looked at the wall. "All these athletes. I didn't know rowing and ice hockey were so popular here in Westbrook. When my kids went to Westbrook High, there definitely weren't rowing and hockey teams."

The secretary said, "Many of our students are referred from Eagle Academy."

"Ah, the private school. That makes sense." She looked again at the pictures. While the secretary took a call, Susan slipped out her phone and took pictures of the wall.

A young man in a business suit stepped off the elevator. He put two stacks of folders on the secretary's desk with sticky notes on the top. Susan glanced at them. 'Yes,' with a smiley face, and 'No.'

Susan stopped the man. "Excuse me, do you teach here?"

He extended his hand. "Carl Silverberg. We refer to ourselves as coaches. I'm stepping in to take over some of the administrative tasks now that Mr. Chambers...I'm sure you saw it on the news."

"We did. We're inquiring about the program. My friend is moving here with her grandson and he's going to be a senior in the fall. Bright boy."

Valerie looked at her then seemed to catch on. She shook his hand. "Valerie Holmes. Yes, Elijah is a genius, but one of those who doesn't conform to rules well. His grades ain't so good and he needs to do well on his SAT's to make up for it."

"We've had fabulous results with our SAT coaching sessions." He grabbed a flyer from the secretary's desk and handed it to her.

"Wow. Not cheap."

He snatched it back. "It's not for everyone."

She snatched it back. "I'm not saying we can't afford it. Elijah's a trust fund baby. Endless well of educational funds thanks to his tycoon dad, may he rest in peace." She made the sign of the cross, although she wasn't Catholic.

"Well then. We offer private sessions, and take care of all the arrangements. Some centers are more conducive to test taking than others."

Susan said, "I thought the kids had to take the test wherever they lived? That's how it was when my kids were in school."

He cleared his throat. "There are extenuating circumstances. We can talk about it if he decides to enroll."

"Thank you," said Valerie. She looked at her watch. "Oops, we'd better go. I've got a real estate deal that needs handling."

Once in the car, Valerie said, "I don't know about you, but my radar went off. A top secret silent partner? Special arrangements for taking the SAT?"

"And all those kids on the crew team on the wall? I don't think Westbrook has a canal big enough to fit them all." Yes, the Hudson River ran through the town, but she was trying to make a point.

"Where are we going for lunch? You promised Lynette you wouldn't skip meals."

"Believe me, I have no intention of skipping lunch. There's a new vegetarian restaurant out by the university, or we can blow our diets and go to the deli around the corner."

"Vegetarian sounds good."

When they arrived, the lunch crowd was dissipating and they slid into a wooden booth by the front window. As they waited for their food, Susan looked out the window.

"Hey, isn't that Madison Chambers?"

"Slim, red hair, expensive shoes—that's her. Who's she with?"

He's wearing a suit in this heat and carrying a brief case. My guess is he's an attorney. She must have all kinds of legal stuff to deal with now that her husband is dead."

"She's getting into her car. And he's coming…in here."

The well-dressed man with the brief case slid into a booth behind them. Curious as always, when he picked up his phone, Susan's ears perked up like a puppy hearing the rattle of food hitting his bowl. Valerie leaned against the seat feeling the pressure of the man's back against hers.

He spoke in a stage whisper. "Yeah, I've got all the paperwork drawn up. It all goes in the partner's name. Yes, the off shore account. Okay, send me the confirmation."

The waitress brought two cheese and sprouts sandwiches to the table and set down a basket of sweet potato fries. The fries were gone before either had taken a bite of her sandwich.

Valerie whispered, "What do you think that's about?"

"It sounds like the partner is assuming full ownership of the business and may be hiding some of the profits in an off shore account."

"Doesn't Madison deserve some of the profit? I mean, wouldn't you assume Harold would have left his share of the company to his wife?"

"Maybe whoever the lawyer represents is buying her out, but the partner is making it look like the company is worth less by hiding some of the profits."

"And that lawyer behind us is getting her to sign the contract. Poor Madison. You should ask your father about it. It can't be legal."

"I wish we could get a look at the company's financial records."

"If it's publically traded, you can look at how the stock is doing."

"You know how to do that?"

"I managed an investment banking office for thirty years. I know a thing or two about stocks."

The waitress came by offering refills.

Susan covered her cup with her hand. "If I drink any more ice tea I'll float away. I'll take the check, please."

Valerie said, "This one's on me."

"Nope. My treat. I can't tell you how happy I am to have a like-minded friend my own age move into town. It does get a little lonely with Mike working and the kids have their own busy lives."

"I hear you. My whole life in St. Louis revolves around taking care of Elijah and Jazzy. Jazzy thinks she doesn't need me, but she does."

"A mother is only as happy as her most unhappy child, but is Jazzy unhappy?"

"Not all the time. Jazzy really misses her hubby, but she loves her job and she's always been sort of a loner."

"Then loosen up the reins. New town, new beginning."

"If I didn't see you hovering over Lynette, I'd be more inclined to take your advice."

"What do you mean?"

"She says she's got a full case load, and you step in to try to help. From what I gather, it's not the first time. Maybe we both need to give our daughters space."

She raised her half-empty glass of iced-tea. "To living our own lives. Westbrook better watch out. The dynamic duo is about to hit the streets."

Chapter 11

When they pulled up to the new house, two cars were already parked in the driveway.

Valerie looked at her watch. "We're not late, are we?"

"A little. Let's see how it's going." She and Valerie walked into the living room and saw the inspector heading up the stairs.

The agent stuck her phone back in her purse. "We arrived a little early so I told the inspector to get started. So far things look good. You must be excited with the closing being tomorrow. Are you planning to move in over the weekend?"

Valerie said, "My daughter is coming in for the closing but won't be moving here for a few more weeks. I suppose I can get myself a bit settled before I go back to St. Louis for my things. I was planning on buying a new bed once we got here. Too bad I can't get those shrubs in before Jazzy gets here."

Susan said, "I'll call Carmine and see if they can do it today."

The agent said, "The owners—I mean the previous owners—left in such a hurry, the utilities haven't been turned off. You could get them transferred over and it'll make for a seamless transition. It's a good idea not to leave a house sitting empty too long."

The inspector came down the steps. "Everything's looking good. I'll go out and check the roof and AC unit. The appliances are like new."

The agent said, "I've got another property to show, so I'm going to take off now. Congratulations, once again."

Susan grabbed her phone to call the nursery.

Valerie said, "I'm going to run and look at Elijah's room."

She headed up the stairs and stood in the middle of her grandson's room. Logistically, it was going to be easier living in the same house with Jazzy and Elijah. No more waking Elijah in the middle of the night and driving him to her place when Jazzy had a police emergency. *I'll try and find some bright curtains to match the walls.* Excitement bubbled like lava beneath her skin. Then she heard a noise. Like someone banging on the roof. *Must be the inspector. Hope that roof is good and solid.*

Susan came upstairs. "Let's go bed shopping."

"As soon as the inspector's done."

"He already finished. Took off right after the agent left."

"He's gone?"

"Yeah."

"But I heard him walking around on the roof not five minutes ago."

"Impossible. Maybe it was the wind. Let's go."

Susan and Valerie spent the rest of the afternoon shopping. Susan's feet hurt from all the walking; her wrists hurt from toting bags. While they took a brief break from shopping and plopped into metal chairs outside Starbucks to sip lattes, Valerie called Carmine. After apologizing profusely for his son's behavior the other night, Carmine agreed to do an "emergency landscaping" at a steeply discounted price.

When they got home, Mike had chicken in the oven and vegetables in the microwave.

Susan kissed his neck. "Thanks for getting dinner started."

"I made plenty. Hope Jazmin and Elijah didn't eat dinner on the plane."

Susan laughed. "Dinner? They'll be lucky if they get a bag of peanuts. Hope they didn't pack their own Snacky Sax. Sorry, that was a bad joke."

Mike shook his head. Susan could tell he was trying not to laugh. "I assume the inspection went well?"

Valerie said, "The appliances are practically new, the AC is functional, and we won't be needing a new roof any time soon. I bought a bed. Maybe tomorrow night Elijah and I will camp out at the new place."

"Are you sure Jazmin doesn't want to crash on our sofa instead of staying at a hotel?"

"Thanks, Mike, but I think she's looking forward to some quiet time and maid service." She looked at the clock. "She should be here soon."

"I just got a message from Carmine Vitulli. They finished planting the shrubs."

"I can't wait to see," said Valerie.

The doorbell rang. Susan said, "That must be them. Just in time." She flung open the door. "Welcome to Westbrook."

"Something smells good." Jazmin bent over and kissed Susan's cheek. She had the same deep set eyes, mocha skin, and warm smile as her mother.

Susan said, "We were just getting dinner on the table. I'll bet you two are starving."

Elijah attached himself to Valerie. "I missed you, sweety. Wait until you see your new room. And there's a swing set in the back yard."

Susan said, "Come sit. Dinner's ready." Mike took the chicken out of the oven while she grabbed a pitcher of iced tea from the fridge.

"Mom, we can't wait to see the new house. I hope it's as great as it looked in the pictures."

"Even better," said Valerie. "The closing is bright and early so we'll have the rest of the day to pick up a few things."

"We both have apartments full of stuff already. I'm not sure we need anything."

"I'm thinking new curtains for Elijah's room, a couple of trash cans—I'm treating myself to a new bathroom set."

"And don't forget a broom," said Susan. "And does Elijah have a bike?"

Elijah's eyes lit up. "Can I get a bike, Mom?"

"One step at a time." She took a bite of chicken. "By the way, how's Lynette holding up?"

"She's got her hands full. I'm sure Valerie told you about it."

"What are the odds the two of you would be sitting on either side of a dead passenger?"

"A *poisoned* passenger," said Valerie.

"Last I checked with Lynette, she wasn't convinced it was murder."

"I think she is now. But, let's not talk about it with my grandson here. How's your chicken, Elijah?"

"It's good. Do you have dessert?"

Susan put her hands on her hips. "Does a duck quack? Of course, we have dessert. Do you like chocolate chip ice cream? With hot fudge and whipped cream?"

Elijah mirrored her hand on the hips stance. "Does a dog bark?" He had his grandmother's smile.

Susan loved his little dimples and how his front teeth looked too big for his mouth. She scooped out the ice cream and Elijah licked every last drop from the bowl. She wondered if having a grandson was much different than having a granddaughter.

With dessert dishes piled in the sink, Elijah busied himself rustling a fishing toy in front of Johann. Ludwig was out of sight, probably under the bed. They brought Jazmin up to speed on the case. Susan wasn't sure if she took them seriously or was just amusing herself, pretending to listen.

"So, you ruled out the son because he didn't enter the house, but the father is still a suspect?"

"He spent a fortune he didn't have sending his son to the prep academy and after all that, he wasn't accepted. The son must have worried that daddy was angry enough to do something drastic, or else why follow him to the Chambers' house?"

"Here's my biggest question. How would this man know Harold was packing Snacky Stix for his trip? And where did he come up with cyanide?"

Susan couldn't resist correcting her. "Snacky Sax. Not Snaky Stix." The part about knowing Harold would pack those for the plane bothered her, too. She ignored the question and plowed on. "He owns a nursery with an apple orchard. With twenty or so apples you can crush up seeds to make enough cyanide to kill someone. I looked it up on the internet."

"And don't forget about the fertilizer," added Valerie. "But according to our source, it's difficult to extract cyanide from fertilizer."

"Your source? Your cyanide extracting expert source?" Jazmin shook her head in a way Lynette often did when Susan tried to enlighten her. "Well, I think I'm going to call an Uber and head to the hotel. Are you ready, Elijah?"

Susan said, "Don't be silly. We'll drop you off; come on. And we'll pick you up on the way to the closing tomorrow morning. Want to drive by the house tonight?"

"Mom, can we?" said Elijah. "Can we see the swing set?"

"We can drive by, but it's dark outside. We'll see the swing set and the rest of our new house tomorrow."

Mike said, "I'll finish the dishes. Go on."

Jazmin grabbed the two small carry-ons. "Is it far from here?"

"Not at all."

Five minutes into the drive, Susan caught sight of Elijah sleeping in the backseat with his head on Jazmin's lap. When they got to the new house, Susan stopped under a street light at the curb.

Valerie said, "What do you think?"

"So far so good," said Jazmin.

Valerie said, "Wait, what's that?"

"What?" said Jazmin.

"I thought I saw a light in the upstairs window."

"I don't see anything," said Susan.

"Me neither," said Jazmin.

"It...in the upstairs window...I...it must be my imagination."

"Let's get over to the hotel. Elijah's got the right idea. I think we all could use a good night's sleep."

Chapter 12

The next morning, Susan heard Mike rattling around in Evan's old room. She pulled on her robe and peeked in. "What are you doing?"

Mike jumped. "I didn't hear you get up. I told Valerie I'd take Elijah to the park while she and Jazmin closed on the house." He pulled a baseball glove from a box in the closet. "This is about his size, right?"

"And what's the one on the bed?"

"That's for me. I hope Elijah's better at catching a baseball than Annalise."

"Honey, Annalise is five. You'd be better off tossing her a basketball. She'll get there."

"Speaking of getting there, I'm going to run by the hotel and pick up Elijah. I told Valerie I'd drop her and Jazmin off at the closing."

"Then you'd better get moving."

She enjoyed a leisurely breakfast lingering over coffee and the crossword puzzle. Finding herself with a little free time, she scrolled through her phone and looked at the pictures from the 'Wall of Succex.' *Brown, Yale, SUNY Westbrook, SUNY Westbrook...Harvard, SUNY Westbrook...* She looked at the clock on the wall, debating whether or not it was too early to call Janet. *Nonsense. She's on school hours.*

"Janet, I hope I didn't wake you."

"Of course not. I'm an early riser. Everything all right? Is your father okay?"

"Oh, yeah. He's fine. I'm trying to match Westbrook High graduates who attended Succex with last year's freshman class at SUNY Westbrook. I've got three names here." She read them over the phone.

"The first two graduated last year. The last one you mentioned graduated in June."

"Let's start with the ones from last year. This Jessica Darling is pictured playing golf and wearing a Westbrook High team uniform. Did you know her?"

"Yes, and I think she played golf but I'm not sure. Our golf team, I'm afraid to say, doesn't get much attention. Now if it were football, that would be a different story."

"What about Javier Rodriguez? He's pictured in a football helmet. It says he received a full athletic scholarship."

"Javier Rodriguez? No way."

"He wasn't on the team?"

"On the team? Homecoming weekend he was in a car accident. Hit by a drunk driver. Poor kid went through a couple of surgeries and was on and off crutches all year. No way he could have played football."

"Hmmm."

"Are you thinking about what I told you at dinner the other night? About kids getting into colleges because a coach can pull strings?"

"Exactly. Were Javier and Jessica Ivy League material?"

"Solid, but not valedictorians or anything to write home about. I'll tell you one thing. They both come from wealthy families. Rodriguez Hardware—four stores around the county. That's Javier's daddy. And Jessica? Her father is head of surgery at Westbrook Memorial."

"Interesting."

"But how does it help you? Those parents benefitted from Chambers being alive and if the coach was working with Chambers, I'm sure he got a nice kickback for everyone he got into the school."

"The pieces fit together; I know they do."

"Or you're still missing a few pieces."

"Right. I'm going to pick Jason's brain about the coach."

After she hung up, she called Jason and left a voicemail. *I know he teaches a Saturday morning seminar.* Too impatient to wait, she hopped in the car and drove to the university. Although she spotted fewer students on the grounds than during the academic year, Jason had been hired to teach a class or two every summer since he'd been on the faculty. Without the extra income for fertility treatments and Mia's adoption, Susan wouldn't have the privilege of being a grandmother. At least not yet.

"Knock, knock."

A staunch believer in open door policy, Jason's door was only partially shut. He looked up from his desk. "Susan, what are you doing here?"

"I was in the neighborhood and wanted to stop by and see my favorite son-in-law."

"And the real reason?"

"I'm looking for a suspect with a motive to kill Harold Chambers."

"To state the obvious, that's Lynette's job."

"It is. I'm just trying to help out. She's been so busy and short-handed."

"Yeah. There was another robbery last night. The public is putting pressure on the department."

"Well, maybe I can help. Something Janet said made me curious about the football coach."

"The football coach?"

"Yeah. A Westbrook High student who attended Succex was admitted to your freshman class last year on a football scholarship."

"Football is big around here. So what?"

"He spent his entire senior year on crutches, yet I saw his picture plastered on the 'Wall of Succex' in a football jersey."

"I don't know how I can help."

"Can you access students' information?"

"My own students."

"But teaching Freshman English, I'll bet you get a big percentage of the students."

He sighed as if he knew he might as well give in. "Who are we talking about?"

"Javier Rodriguez. And Jessica Darling while you're at it."

Jason clicked the keys on the computer and after a few minutes, said, "I had them both in lecture classes. Can't say I'd recognize either one."

"How were their grades?"

"Javier barely scraped by my class. Jessica got a B."

"Can you pull up the football team roster?"

"Yeah. Give me a minute."

Susan glanced at her watch. Valerie and Jazmin were bound to be done soon. She drummed her fingers on the arm rest while she waited.

"Got it. No Javier Rodriguez listed."

"What's the coach's name?"

"Mark Cullins."

"Do you know him?"

"Sort of. He came by Madison's office a few times."

"To see her?"

"To see Harold. Harold came around to pick Madison up for lunch every Tuesday. Come to think of it…"

"What?"

"Never mind."

"Tell me."

"Lynette would kill me."

Susan assumed a posture that made it clear she wasn't going to back off. "And?"

"Okay, but this better not get back to her."

"Scout's honor."

"I heard arguing a week or two ago on their lunch date day. Madison's door was shut. Harold and Mark Cullins were outside our doors in the hallway arguing with each other. I heard Mark yelling, 'We've got to lay low' and 'back off.' Harold said, 'No way, not now.'"

"He had to be referring to the scholarships," said Susan.

"So Mark Cullins killed Harold because Harold wouldn't back off on faking athletic scholarships? Does that sound like a strong motive to you?" Jason put down the pen he'd been twirling and leaned back in his chair.

"No, but it may not be the whole story."

"Stay out of trouble, Susan. Lynette doesn't need more stress."

"Okay, okay. I've got to go."

When she got back to the car, she read a message from Valerie. The meeting had been delayed and they'd be running later than originally thought. *Maybe I should run over to Madison's and see how she's doing. And what she knows about the coach. After all, I'm in the neighborhood.* She gave Madison a call and headed to her house.

Madison answered the door wearing a terry cloth pair of shorts and a matching top. Her hair was pulled into a neat red pony tail. "Come on in. I was on the way to play tennis, but it can wait."

"I'm glad you're feeling okay."

"I'm trying to stay busy so I don't have time to think about Harold. Physical activity helps. Bad enough I'll be spending all day tomorrow on funeral arrangements. Did you find something?"

"We went out to the nursery. Bruno Vitulli is the one who was in your yard, but according to security cameras, he never entered your place. He was following his father."

"Carmine Vitulli. The one who argued with my husband. The one who had a window of time to tamper with Harold's bag while it was in the foyer."

"Here's the thing. He had to have brought a bag of poisoned Snacky Sax with him to carry out that plan. How on earth would he know Harold would have that particular snack in his bag?"

"You're kidding, right?"

"What do you mean?"

She picked up a photo of her husband with his arm around a young woman. "You know who this is, right? The girl with Harold?"

"Can't say I do."

"It's his daughter, Alissa. She invented Snacky Sax. Didn't you know? He even made a local commercial with his daughter. Haven't you seen it?"

Susan felt as though she'd been punched. *Of course. 'You can relax with Snacky Sax. Locally made. No artificial anything'—with the exception of cyanide.* "I've seen that commercial a thousand times. Harold looked different in person."

"It's amazing what a little make-up and strategic camera angles can do. Harold always carried Snacky Sax with him.

"So he had a daughter. I assume she inherits Succex, or a portion of it, now that he's dead. I assumed you'd be getting it all."

"His daughter doesn't need the company. She has her hands full running her own and Succex is small potatoes compared to her empire."

"So *you* inherited the company?"

"Half of it. The other half goes to his business partner. I wouldn't know the first thing about running a company."

"Who is the partner?"

"I don't know. He insists on remaining anonymous. We've been communicating through an attorney. I'm hoping to unload my shares. The company is hemorrhaging money."

She was about to make a comment about assuming it was succexful, but self-edited. "I was under the impression it was thriving."

"The pool of rich parents trying to get their kids into Ivy League schools is limited here. Westbrook is a small town. Harold had considered moving to the city, but rents in Manhattan are ridiculous. They planned to start advertising heavily in Westchester and Rockland counties this fall. Those communities are close enough that it wasn't too far of a stretch to get the kids here."

"Do you think the business partner, whoever it is, had a motive to kill Harold? Maybe they weren't on the same page about the company's direction."

"I never heard Harold mention any tensions between him and his partner."

"What about someone who worked for Harold? I hear he worked closely with the coach, Mark Cullins, at SUNY Westbrook."

"Well, come to think of it, I overheard Harold and the coach arguing outside my office door not long ago when Harold came by to pick me up for lunch. I was on a call so my door was closed but I heard Mark say something like 'back off. I asked Harold about it and he said something about not seeing eye to eye."

"A difference of opinion?"

"I heard Harold say, 'I'm going to dump you, you unappreciative bastard.' I was trying to be delicate. They started out as good friends. Coach and his girlfriend came over for dinner a few times. It's only recently things changed."

"Did he have the opportunity to plant the poison snacks before the trip?"

"No, but the two of them were back and forth in each other's offices all the time. Harold kept boxes of Snacky Sax everywhere—his office, our home, the car."

"So he could have planted it at the office and it wound up in his travel bag. I guess it wouldn't matter where Harold ate the poison, the end result would be the same." She looked at Madison's sad face. "I'm sorry. I didn't mean to be so blunt."

"It's okay. I know you're trying to help. It's more than I'm getting from the police these days."

Something nagged at Susan. "How would the coach get access to cyanide? Does he teach Chemistry or have access to a lab?"

"No, but his son works at the shipping department at Agrowmex."

Susan's pulse quickened. "They ship fresh fruits and vegetables. Like apples. And apple seeds can be turned into cyanide. Did you mention all this to the police?"

"Like I said, when I've tried to call and talk to someone, I get stuck on hold."

"I'm going straight to my daughter with this. They're going to catch your husband's killer."

"I hope so." She picked up her tennis racket from the back of the sofa. "I'd better get going. I appreciate your help more than I can express."

Susan looked at her messages. Valerie and Jazmin were finished and ready to be picked up. Would Lynette take this new suspect seriously or brush it off as speculation? All she could say was that there was tension between Harold and the coach, and Harold planned to fire him. And everyone seemed to know

about Harold's daughter and his penchant for eating
Snack Sax. Everyone but her.

Chapter 13

Susan spotted Valerie and Jazmin outside when she pulled up to the mortgage office. She rolled down the window. "I'm here to pick up a couple of new home owners. Have you seen them?"

Valerie held up the keys. "You're looking at them. Signed, sealed, and delivered."

Jazmin said, "What are we waiting for? Can I see my new home now?"

Susan pushed the speed limit while Jazmin and Valerie discussed the logistics of the move. She wanted to ask Jazmin about doing a background check on the coach, but this wasn't the right moment.

Valerie pointed out the window. "There it is. It's got curb appeal, right?"

"And those shrubs by the front door—they weren't in the photos you sent."

"Just had them installed yesterday but it was dark when we drove by last night. We need to buy some of those pretty tile numbers for the front door. I've been looking on Amazon."

Jazmin got out of the car. "First things first. Where's that key?"

Valerie opened the front door. Jazmin was silent as she went in and out of the downstairs rooms. "Well? Please don't say you hate it."

"It's gorgeous. So much space. I want to check out the upstairs."

While Jazmin went upstairs, Susan told Valerie about her conversation with Madison Chambers.

"Before Lynette tells me I'm a meddling fool, do you suppose Jazmin would run a background check on Mark Cullins? And the daughter. Even if she is rich, it's hard to believe she wouldn't be a little miffed by being excluded from her father's will."

Jazmin came down the steps. "Mom, you did great. Elijah's going to flip when he sees the stars on the ceiling in his new room."

"My new bed is being delivered this afternoon. What if Elijah and I camp out here tonight? Think he'd like that?"

"I'm sure he'd be thrilled, but his bed isn't here yet."

Susan said, "I've got a sleeping bag at home. Evan liked to camp when he was in high school."

"Okay. I'll use the evening to take a swim, read a book, and order room service."

Susan said, "Your mom and I are trying to help Lynette find suspects for the murder case. I have a lead. Mrs. Chambers, the victim's widow, said Harold and the SUNY Westbrook coach argued and talked about parting ways. Jason, Lynette's husband, said he heard them arguing as well."

"It's up to Lynette to interview him. I'm not going to step on her toes and I don't have jurisdiction here anyway."

"Not yet but soon you will. All I was hoping for was a background check. Before I run to Lynette with this. If the man turns out to be a saint, I'll drop it."

"I suppose. Just a background check."

"Thanks, Jazmin."

"Didn't you say there was an outlet mall around here? I'm in a shopping mood."

"My Jazzy asking to go to a mall? That's not something you hear every day. What happened to not needing anything?"

"I'm excited and if I pick up a few things, it's less I'll have to pack. Speaking of which, I'll call the movers later and nail down a date."

The mall buzzed with shoppers. Susan couldn't resist picking up a few throw pillows and some cute sundresses for Annalise and Mia. Jazmin bought more than either of them—a new set of everyday dishes from the Corelle shop, a suitcase from the Samsonite outlet, and a floral tote bag, more feminine than Susan thought Jazmin would choose, from the Vera Bradley store. By the time they carried armloads of bags to Susan's trunk, her neck and shoulders ached, not to mention her feet. When they arrived at her house, Valerie carried a small bag in with her.

Elijah ran to the door and whined. "Mommy, you said you'd let me see the house and you were gone all day."

"Sorry, honey. I bet you had fun at the park. How would you like to camp out with Grandma in your new house tonight?"

Elijah hugged Jazmin. "Yeah! Can I go on the swings? Can we get a dog?"

"Swings, yes. Dog? I'll have to think about it."

Valerie pulled a bathing suit from the bags. "Look, Elijah. Want to go swimming?"

"Yeah. Thanks, Grandma." He took the swim trunks and held them against his waist.

"The previous owners left one of those plastic wading pools in the backyard and we can set up the sprinklers."

They ordered pizza, and after dinner, Susan dropped Jazmin off at the hotel and Valerie and Elijah at the new house. When she got back, Mike suggested watching a movie. She cuddled next to him on the sofa.

"Do you think Harold Chambers' daughter killed her father?"

"I thought we were watching a movie?"

"We are. I was just wondering if she can be completely ruled out. She's rich, but Harold was her father."

"I can't imagine why she'd be mad if she's as rich as you say she is. Now quiet or we'll miss what's going on."

After a while, Mike fell asleep next to her. Susan carefully extricated herself from the sofa and opened her lap top, then searched for info on Alissa Chambers. Everything seemed as Madison said. *She's a billionaire. Her dad made two commercials with her. She and her father started a foundation to provide scholarships to underprivileged high school seniors. A foundation? Madison said his company was bleeding money so how would he have money to start a scholarship foundation? Maybe it was a tax write-off?*

Mike stirred. "Hey, what happened to the movie?"

"The detective had a showdown with the serial killer and shot him in the head."

"I thought we were watching a romantic comedy?"

"Just testing you." She gave him a kiss. "Speaking of romantic, are you ready for bed?"

She took his hand and led him up the steps.

*****

Valerie and Elijah settled in at the house. Almost immediately, they headed outside at Elijah's insistence. Valerie filled the pool and sat on a crushed box. She'd have to see about picking up some lawn chairs.

As dusk approached, Valerie swatted at a mosquito that landed on her arm. "Elijah, honey, it's getting dark out. Why don't we go inside and play cards before bed?"

He stepped out of the pool, shivering. Valerie cuddled him in an over-sized beach towel they'd bought at the mall. "Can we make popcorn?"

"We don't have groceries, but I bought some cookies at the mall earlier and I was saving them to share with you."

"Okay, Grandma." He ran into the house, followed by Valerie. Just before going in the sliding glass door, Valerie bent down and picked up a foil fast-food wrapper. *Where did this come from? I didn't see this the other day.*

"Grandma, I'm cold."

"Coming, honey. Want to take a bath in the new bath tub? You'll be the first in our family."

"Yep. Then cookies, right?"

"You bet."

Valerie got Elijah settled in the tub and walked into his room planning how to best arrange the furniture when it came. She heard a sound outside, like something scraping against the house and peeked out the window but it had gotten too dark to see anything. *I'm guessing there's an outdoor light, but I can't leave Elijah up here by himself.* She heard another sound, like the one she heard the other day. Like something banging on the roof.

"Grandma, I want to get out of the tub."

"Coming, honey! At eight, he was old enough to get out by himself but she didn't mind. She grabbed one of the thick new towels she'd picked up at the mall earlier. "So, how's the new tub?"

"Great. Is Mommy going to use this bathroom, too?"

"Nope. She has one in her room, so it's all yours. You're going to keep it nice and clean, right?"

"Yep."

They ate cookies and played Old Maid. Elijah got more cookie crumbs on the floor than in his mouth. When it was time for bed, she laid out the sleeping bag in her room downstairs next to the bed. It wasn't long before Elijah abandoned the camping idea and climbed into bed next to her.

During the night, Valerie woke up in a cold sweat. She could have sworn she heard her dead husband whispering, "Be careful." She clutched the covers up to her neck and looked at Elijah sleeping so soundly. Then she trembled. *What if our new house is haunted?*

Chapter 14

Mike piled his breakfast dishes in the sink while Susan worked on the crossword puzzle from the newspaper.

Mike said, "I mapped out a little tour of the town. What time are we supposed to start sight-seeing?"

"I told Valerie we'd pick them up at nine. After that, we'll swing by the hotel and get Jazmin." What's that Hawaiian goose again?"

"Nene. N-E-N-E"

"Thanks. Done." She got up and poured food into the cat bowls. "I wonder if Elijah's going to get that dog he wants. I know Valerie loves animals."

"I doubt it's the first thing on Jazmin's mind, but they have a yard, right?"

"Yes, they do."

"It's almost nine now. Ready to go?"

"I'll text Valerie and tell her we're on the way."

After gathering the passengers, Mike drove by Elijah's future school, the library, the skating rink, and the community center.

Mike said, "They've got t-ball, little league, karate lessons—you name it. Elijah's got an arm on him."

A little voice from the back seat said, "I'm on the Pirates."

Jazmin said, "The season will be finishing soon back home. When we get settled we can look into some activities."

Susan said, "Mike, drive by the park."

When they neared the entrance, a mass of cars filled the roadside and Susan spotted runners with numbers pinned to their shirts. "They must be having a race." She opened the window and looked out. "There's a sign. It's a 5K scholarship run. Look Elijah. See the finish line with the clock over it? It lets the runners know how fast they went."

Mike said, "Should I park or move on?"

"Yeah, park. We can walk over to the monkey bars from here."

Elijah ran ahead with Valerie on his tail. Jazmin caught up to Susan after snapping a few photos with her phone. Then she took Susan aside.

"I ran a background check on the coach, Mark Cullins. He has an arrest record."

"I knew it. Was it a violent crime? Could he have it in him to commit murder?" asked Susan.

"No, it was a white collar crime. Skimming funds. I'm surprised they hired him at the university. No holding people up at gun point or anything. And there's a gap in his teaching history."

"What did he do in the meantime? Was he in jail?" Susan wrung her hands together in anticipation of a juicy tidbit.

"That's where it gets interesting. He got off with a fine. Then he worked for a small college prep company in Connecticut."

"Like Succex?"

"Yes. And the name of record listed as his boss? "Jazmin paused like an actor before delivering a vital line. "Harold Chambers."

"Wow. That can't be a coincidence. But I was under the impression Succex has been here a while."

"Opened five years ago. Shortly after Chambers declared bankruptcy and hastily closed the Connecticut business." Jazmin glanced toward the monkey bars.

"What about the parents who paid him to work with their kids?"

"They lost out with the bankruptcy." Jazmin started walking toward the playground.

Susan followed her. "Motive for murder?"

"I don't know. They'd have had to track him down to Westbrook, and it's been a few years. Plus, those parents had to have enough disposable income to pay that tuition." Jazmin kicked a stone out of her path.

"Why would Chambers hire Cullins to work at the new business when he was skimming from the old one?"

"Think about it. What if the two of them worked together? Did you notice the shirts on those runners we passed?"

"No."

Jazmin stopped for a moment. "It said the Harrison Foundation."

"And you think that's the foundation Harold and Cullins ran?"

"It's just a hunch. I'm positive it's a non-profit organization and if I'm right, Cullins was a valuable asset. He knew how to skim money away from the company and hide it in the foundation so Chambers didn't have to get his hands dirty. I've seen it before. And Chambers got his attorneys to make sure Cullins got off without jail time." Jazmin continued walking.

"And with his job as a coach, he knew how to fake athletic scholarships. Both Jason and Chamber's wife said Harold and Cullins argued. Cullins said something about laying low and backing off. Harold didn't agree." She looked over her shoulder and noticed Mike had just about caught up to them.

Jazmin said, "Maybe he was afraid they were going to get caught. When Chambers didn't agree, Cullins killed him to save his own hide. A second arrest for stealing would certainly land him jail time."

"I thought you were going to spend the night reading and relaxing? You've been busy."

Valerie ran to them, carrying her grandson. "Elijah's already had enough monkey bars. He fell and scraped his knee."

Jazmin said, "I've got band aids and wipes. Let's take a look. Does it hurt, honey?"

Elijah wiped away tears. "No."

Jazmin kissed her finger and touched it to his knee. "All better?"

Valerie said, "That's my brave boy. How about we get lunch? Maybe Miss Susan and Mr. Mike know a good pizza place."

Vito's Pizza. The aroma of oregano leaked out the door. Valerie insisted on a pizzeria so Jazmin and Elijah could try authentic New York style pizza. Elijah didn't quite get the hang of folding the droopy slice and saucy cheese plopped on his lap. Jazmin patted at it with a napkin, then cut up the rest for him. When they finished lunch, Jazmin took Elijah back to the hotel. Susan filled Valerie in on the conversation she'd had with Jazmin at the park.

Susan said, "I'm going to call Madison Chambers and see if Coach Cullins stopped by the house the night before the trip." She picked up her phone to call but didn't get an answer. A few minutes later, Madison called her back. Susan put the phone on speaker.

"I didn't recognize the number at first" said Madison. "Did you find out something?"

"Did you know Coach Cullins and your husband worked together in Connecticut before you all moved to Westbrook?"

"No, I didn't. I wouldn't. Harold and I were just married last year. He never mentioned another business and honestly, I didn't know he lived in Connecticut. I guess there were a lot of things I didn't know."

"What do you mean?"

"Nothing, really. We had rather a whirlwind romance. We were so busy with the present, we didn't discuss the past."

"Was Cullins at your house the night Carmine and Bruno came by?" asked Susan.

"No."

Susan felt herself wilt. She thought she'd been onto something with Mark Cullins having motive. *Cullins could have switched the Snacky Sax out earlier.*

Madison continued. "But he was with him in the morning. He drove him to the airport. Mark called late the night before. I heard them arguing on the phone. Then Harold said I didn't need to drive him to the airport in the morning. Mark was going to do it because they had 'things to discuss.' I'd forgotten with all the grief I've been dealing with."

When she hung up, Valerie said, "Coach Cullins was with Harold Chambers the morning he left for St. Louis. That makes him the last person in Westbrook to see him, right?"

"Yep. He said he had things to discuss with Harold."

"What things?"

"I don't know. There was the comment about laying low earlier. Maybe Coach Cullins was afraid someone was on to them. If he was caught falsely accepting students based on needing them for a team, he'd go to jail."

"Wouldn't that implicate Chambers as well?"

"Chambers could have pretended to know nothing about it. Could have pinned it all on Coach Cullins."

"Staying out of jail would be worth risking a murder charge?"

"He has a criminal record already. He had a lot at stake."

"Where would he get the cyanide?"

"I'm going to find out." She sat down with her laptop and scrolled through Google. "This is ridiculous. You can buy cyanide on the web." She combed through the information. "Get this. A teenager bought potassium chloride over the internet using his mother's credit card and spiked his friend's drink, killing him."

"No way. Why is cyanide for sale on the internet?"

"I saw something in here about legitimate use as rat poison and in film developing."

"You have to tell Lynette."

Susan picked up the phone, bracing herself for Lynette's annoyance. "Lynette? I hate to bother you but there's something you need to know."

"What is it? Is it Dad? Is it his heart again?"

"No, nothing like that. We found out that a Mark Cullins, coach at SUNY Westbrook, drove Harold Chambers to the airport and was most likely the last person to see him before he left. The coach and Harold argued about whether or not to lay low. Seems like the coach arranged false athletic scholarships to get Succex students into SUNY Westbrook."

"Mom…"

"Jazzy said Coach Cullins has an arrest record for white collar crimes. Also, he worked with Chambers back in Connecticut at a company similar to Succex. It went bankrupt and closed down."

"Jazmin is in on this?"

"We asked for her help. We knew how busy you've been."

"I already interviewed Cullins. I know about his record, and his former association with Chambers. I told you I'd handle this."

"Did you know you can order cyanide over the internet?"

"Mom, why don't you and Valerie do something fun, like go see a movie? I've got it under control. After the press conference we'll see what goes down."

"Press conference?"

"You didn't know? Mark Cullins called a press conference. They're supposed to make an announcement."

"An announcement? About the silent partner?"

"Did you ever consider Mark Cullins might *be* the silent partner?"

"And if Madison sold him her shares of the company, he'd have control of it all."

Chapter 15

Susan grabbed her phone and called Madison Chambers. "Do you have any idea what Mark Cullins wants to announce at the press conference today?"

"Susan? I have no idea, really. Mark asked me to be there. When I asked him why he said it was a surprise. I have a feeling he's going to announce a scholarship fund in Harold's name."

"And what about the silent partner? Do you suppose he'll be there?"

"He's been in the shadows all this time. I can't see him coming forward now."

"Do you suppose Mark Cullins is the silent partner? They worked together back in Connecticut."

"I don't know. Come to think of it, Mark bought himself a Tesla last year. I did wonder how he managed it on a coach's salary. And I've run into him at my tennis club. Memberships aren't cheap."

"You heard him arguing with Harold, right? You said Mark wanted to give him a ride to the airport so they could talk."

"But I inherited Harold's share of the business when he died. Even with Harold out of the picture, Mark isn't in control of the company."

"Did he ask to buy your shares?"

"No, though he did say something about wanting to get together to talk next week."

"What if you *offered* to sell him your shares? If we record him admitting he's the silent partner, then I can go to Lynette and show he had a motive. Unless you have interest in running the company?"

"I don't know the first thing about running a company. Wouldn't Mark be suspicious? Why would I offer to sell my shares to an employee? Should I say I suspect he's the silent partner?"

"Never mind; this isn't a good idea. He may be a murderer."

"I'll tread carefully. I'll set up a meeting and get back to you."

"Are you sure? Make it a public place."

"Will do."

Valerie said, "I checked out Succex. It looks like the company is on financial thin ice. I confirmed with a broker friend."

"And if the company got into legal trouble, that'd be the end of them. So if Harold wanted to keep doing what they were doing or ramp it up to improve their financial health, and Cullins wanted to back off, there's conflict."

"Big enough stakes for murder?" Valerie plopped down on the sofa next to Susan.

"It's that, or Carmine Vitulli's anger over Bruno not getting into Harvard. So far, that's all we've got."

"For Heaven's sake, Carmine Vitulli tends flowers for a living. I can't picture him as a murderer."

"Remember what I said about killers."

"Yeah. All of Ted Bundy's neighbors loved him. Anyhow, do you mind if we run by the new house? I want to measure the area over the bed to see if the rug I've got hanging back home will be big enough to cover the wall."

"Sure." She told Mike they'd be out for a while.

When they got to the house, Valerie made a beeline for her new room and whipped out a tape measure.

"Susan, hold the end so I can measure this wall."

Susan held the end as Valerie stretched it across. "What's the verdict?"

"I think it will center perfectly. The dresser will go over by the door with Elijah's school picture hanging over it."

"Anything else while we're here?"

"I want to check out the back yard. I think I saw a few bare patches over by the fence." She opened the sliding door and Susan followed her over to the fence.

"You're right. You just need some grass seeds or a few patches of sod and it will be fine."

Susan peeked into the neighbor's yard where a woman close to her own age was reading a book in a lounge chair. The woman caught her eye and came over to the fence.

"You must be the new neighbors. I heard the place was sold."

Valerie said, "I'll be living here with my daughter and grandson. They're flying home tomorrow to pack up. My daughter, Jazzy, is a detective."

"Wonderful. I hear there was a second bank robbery the other day. I don't know what this town's coming to."

Susan said, "We have so little crime here." *Outside of a couple of murders, that is.*

"Well, it'll be nice having a detective as a back fence neighbor. I think I caught a glimpse of your grandson."

"Really? When?"

"Well, I saw the kitchen light go on a few times, and the other day a young man was out in the yard. Wasn't that your grandson?"

"No, my grandson is eight. Are you sure it wasn't the previous owner?"

"Oh, no. They're gone. One day I see a *For Sale* sign in the yard; the next day a moving truck pulls up. Not even a goodbye. And I considered us friends."

"Why do you think they left in such a hurry?" said Susan.

"You got me. I thought maybe a sick parent or a new job but you don't pack up and move overnight like that, right?"

Susan said, "If it was a sick parent, I'd think they'd have hustled to be with them—but sell the house overnight?"

"And they'd just put in the swing set. They sure doted on their little boy. They were always out in the yard when the weather was nice. See the sandbox over by the patio? They put that in when they first bought the house. April had just found out she was pregnant."

"How old is their son?"

"He was going to start kindergarten, so I'd say five. Cute as a button."

Valerie said, "Then you've lived here a while?"

"We've been in this house thirty years. You're going to love the neighborhood."

Valerie said, "Can you alert me if you see anyone in or around the house again? I'll give you my number and Susan's too in case it happens while I'm back in St. Louis packing."

"You bet. I'm Clara by the way. My husband is Tom. He's out on the golf course like he is most weekends."

"Valerie Holmes. You'll have to come by when we get settled."

She and Susan inspected the grass once again.

"Do you think this is from digging? I wonder if they had a dog."

Susan bent down and ran her hand over the dirt. "Maybe."

"Weird how the Russells took off in such a hurry. They weren't even present at the closing. All the paperwork went through their attorney."

Susan looked at her watch. "We should get back so we can have dinner before the press conference airs."

Valerie started toward the house, then noticed a flattened French fry box behind a bush.

"Someone's been eating out here. I know I didn't see this when I was out here with Elijah and the ketchup smear ain't even crusty yet."

"I think you should look into getting a security system."

"Like I've got money for that? I'll have the locks changed though. Come on, let's go."

Chapter 16

Jazmin brought Chinese takeout over to Susan's for dinner. Elijah, determined to eat lo-mien with chop sticks, had gotten more on the floor than in his mouth. He refused the fork Susan offered him.

"He's stubborn, just like Jazzy," said Valerie.

"I prefer to say determined, Mom. And look who's talking? Who do you think we got it from?"

Mike wandered into the living room and turned on the TV. "The press conference is about to start."

They carried their plates into the living room, except for Elijah. Jazmin made it clear he wasn't to start strewing noodles all over the living room carpet.

"There's Madison and the press. Where's Coach Cullins?" said Susan.

"Late for his own press conference? It's not reflecting well on the company," said Jazmin.

When it was clear he wasn't going to show up, Madison said a few words about Succex continuing on in Harold's memory, but admitted she didn't know what the big announcement was and apologized for the no show before climbing down from the podium.

Valerie said, "That's awfully weird. Do you think she had a chance to meet with Cullins beforehand?"

"Let's find out."

Mike said, "Give the woman a chance to get back to her car at least."

Jazmin said, "What meeting?"

Valerie said, "She was going to talk to Coach Cullins about selling her shares in the company to him. We think Cullins could be the silent partner."

"Because…"

Susan took over. "He and Harold weren't seeing eye to eye over the direction of the business. You told us Mark Cullins had an arrest record and we thought maybe…"

Jazmin said, "You should have gone to Lynette. I thought you told me you were going to do that?"

Valerie said, "We did but she wasn't amenable to our help."

"Mom, you've got to stop right here and now. You can't be butting into police business." She turned to Susan. "And you have to stop encouraging her."

Boy, have I heard that conversation before. She felt relieved when her phone vibrated. "It's Madison. I'll be right back." She walked outside onto their back porch.

"Did you see the press conference? He was a no show."

"Calm down, Madison. Were you able to meet with him earlier?"

"No. I arranged for us to meet at the tennis club. When I got there, I didn't see him. I waited, then I tried to call him, but no luck. I figured maybe I could catch him in front of Succex before the press conference but you see how that turned out. I'll bet he left town."

"All right. I'll call Lynette with our theory and tell her, I mean suggest to her, that he most likely skipped town. I'll get back to you if I have any news."

When she got to the bottom of the stairs, Jazmin and Elijah were standing by the door.

"Elijah and I are going back to the hotel. He's had a busy day. I called an Uber."

When the door locked behind them, Susan said, "Guess it's just us for coffee and dessert."

Valerie said, "Maybe you *should* call Lynette. Jazmin's going to tell her everything anyway."

Susan sighed. "I'm sure you're right." She punched in Lynette's number. "Honey, I have something to discuss with you. It's about Mark Cullins."

"Mark Cullins? I'm a little busy right now."

"Yes, Mark Cullins. Madison, Valerie, and I have reason to believe he's the silent partner and he killed Harold to gain control of the company."

"Really? I'll ask him. He's here with me now. Oops, he's not answering. Guess that's because he's dead."

"What!"

"I'm at the crime scene waiting for the medical examiner."

"So you don't know for sure?"

"Oh, he's dead all right."

"Where are you?"

"At the tennis club. I've got to go."

Susan put away the phone. She felt her head whirling like a rogue helicopter. "Coach Cullins is dead."

"What? We were so sure he murdered Harold Chambers. Now what?"

"Back to the drawing board."

Mike said, "No to the drawing board. Don't the two of you have anything better to focus on?"

Valerie said, "I was thinking of flying home with Jazzy and Elijah tomorrow. The sooner I pack, the quicker I can move into my new house. Even if Jazzy has to stay in St. Louis a bit longer, Elijah's on summer break. We can get settled."

"Summer break," said Mike. "We could use a vacation."

Susan said, "You don't have any vacation time. You used it while you were recovering."

"True, but you're retired. You can do as you please. Why don't you fly back with Valerie and help her pack? It would give you a chance to visit with Evan and Cara again."

"I don't know. It costs money."

Valerie said, "I'm using the voucher from the airline. It was nice how they compensated us for sitting next to a dead man."

"I forgot about the voucher. You know what? I'm in. I'll give Evan a call right now."

"Make sure you can get on the flight, first," said Mike.

Susan took care of the arrangements, called Evan, and threw some clothes into a suitcase. While they were in St. Louis, perhaps she and Valerie could nose around at the conference hotel where the college showcase convention took place. What was Harold Chambers doing there, anyway? And maybe the poisoned Snacky Sax didn't come from Westbrook at all. Perhaps it came from St. Louis.

Chapter 17

The plane ride was decidedly less eventful than the previous one. Susan and Valerie arrived in St. Louis after dark and piled into an Uber.

"It's every bit as sticky and hot as it is in New York," said Susan. She couldn't wait for a cool shower and a soft bed. The driver had the windows open rather than turning on the AC and she felt nauseated. "I can barely breathe in this car."

"Don't worry. I keep it nice and cold in my place. Are you okay? Do you need a snack?"

"I'm good. Just hot." She closed her eyes trying to doze, but the Uber driver needed a lesson on working a manual clutch. Stop, jerk, stop, go. She was relieved when she felt the car stop for good.

The Uber had pulled in front of a small apartment building on a quiet, tree-lined street dotted with antique lamp posts. *Pine Boulevard. What an appropriate name.* She followed Valerie up the stairs, tugging her suitcase behind her.

"Home sweet home." Valerie flipped on the lights. "You can see my apartment is tiny but the sofa pulls out into a bed and I hear it's pretty comfortable. It's better than paying for a hotel."

"Yeah. Figures I'd come when Cara's parents are in town and have dibs on Evan and Cara's guest room." She looked around the apartment. "It looks like you already started packing."

"I bought some boxes and I've been getting rid of what I don't need. Too much stuff just weighs you down."

"And the more room you have, and the longer you're in a place, the more you accumulate. I wouldn't know where to start if Mike and I ever moved."

Valerie grabbed a set of linens from the linen closet, then removed the cushions from the floral sofa.

"Let me help you." She grabbed one side of the sofa and pulled. "I was so sure Coach Cullins murdered Chambers."

"You brought that conference program Jason got in the mail, right?"

"Yeah. We can see which colleges were there, specifically Ivy Leagues, and maybe someone at the hotel will remember him."

"Slim chance. Must have been hundreds at the convention." Valerie tucked the fitted sheet around the thin mattress.

"Well, we'll figure something out. And I promise we will leave time for packing." She let out a yawn.

"Get some sleep. Goodnight," said Valerie. She flipped off the lights on her way to her bedroom.

Susan slept through the night without so much as a bathroom trip. The next morning, they stopped at Whole Foods for breakfast muffins and coffee while they waited for the worst of rush hour to pass. Then Valerie pointed out Forest Park, Barnes Jewish Hospital, and some of her favorite restaurants on the way down town. She found a metered parking spot in front of the convention center. "The hotel is right across the street."

They hustled to the hotel entrance when the pedestrian light turned to white. Valerie said, "This is going to be a tough one. Where do we start?"

Susan marched right up to the check-in desk, deliberately choosing an employee who looked barely old enough to shave.

"Excuse me. I was wondering if you could help me. My hubby was here for that college showcase and he thinks he left his tweed jacket behind. I'm in town visiting my son and I said I'd give it a shot. Worth a try, right? He bought that jacket on our Scotland trip last year so it has sentimental value."

"I'll check the lost and found." He disappeared behind a door.

"You know it ain't gonna be there," said Valerie.

"Just play along."

A few minutes later, the man reappeared empty-handed. "I'm sorry but no tweed jackets in there."

"Can you maybe see what room he was in? Perhaps the maid missed it or thought it belonged to the current guest."

"What's his name?"

"Harold Chambers."

He fiddled on the keyboard, the said, "Got it. He stayed in a king suite on the thirteenth floor."

"Can you check with whoever cleans that floor?"

A line had formed behind them.

"I can't. There's a cat fancier's convention starting this morning and as you can see, we're a little busy. Maybe later."

Susan thanked him and headed toward the elevator. "It's just after checkout time and with a crowd coming in, I'll bet whoever cleans the floor is up there now. Come on."

"I thought hotels didn't have thirteenth floors?"

"Maybe they shouldn't. Was a bit unlucky for Harold Chambers, I'd say."

With a ding, the door to the glass elevator slid open. Susan lost her patience when it stopped at every floor.

"Figures we missed the express," said Susan. On the next floor, a maid pushing a cart full of cleaning supplies and linens squeezed in and rode to the thirteenth floor with Valerie, and Susan.

"He stayed in Room 1310." Susan checked the directional tile on the wall. "This way."

Valerie followed her down the hall. "Now what?" They stood in front of Room 1310. "Do we knock?"

Squeaky wheels rolled down the hallway. The maid from the elevator stopped and slid her key card in 1310.

"Excuse me," said Susan. "My husband was here last week in this room and I think he left his tweed jacket in the closet. Did you happen to notice it?"

"A tweed jacket? No, I didn't see it. If I had, I would have brought it down to lost and found."

"Do you remember my husband? He was...he's overweight with a beard and blue eyes. In his mid to late fifties?"

"No, ma'am. I have little contact with the guests." She looked down the hall. "See the young man in the khaki uniform picking up the tray in front of that door? He does room service. Maybe he saw him, but I'm sure there wasn't a tweed jacket in that room."

"Thank you." Susan waited until the maid went inside 1312, then whispered, "Let's go."

They strolled down the hall, Valerie making a point to nearly run smack into the employee. "I'm so sorry. I left my glasses at home."

"No problem."

Susan said, "I wonder if you can help me. My husband was here last week in Room 1310. Overweight, middle aged, with a beard? He came home with stomach issues. He's supposed to be following a strict gluten-free diet but I'm sure he cheated. The doctors want to run all kinds of expensive tests, but if he'd just admit to eating gluten, they could skip the tests and send him home to wait it out."

"Well, I did deliver several meals to that room. I know who you're talking about. I brought them a continental breakfast every morning."

"Them?" said Susan.

The man turned red and fidgeted. "I never should have said that."

"It's okay. I was sure he was cheating on me. If I get proof, I'll come out of the divorce in better shape. What did she look like?"

"I shouldn't."

Valerie said, "You know, you remind me of my son. My son would have his knickers in a knot if his daddy cheated on me. Taking advantage of a poor old lady? It's just not right. My friend here is going to be out on the street with his fancy lawyers handling the divorce and all."

Susan said, "I won't tell anyone you spoke to me. I'm going to scrape together the money for a private investigator but only if I know for sure. If I can prove he was cheating…"

He fidgeted, and glanced up and down the empty hallway. "Okay. He was with a much younger woman. Blonde hair. Rude. They both were. And cheap. Barely even a tip."

"And he can certainly afford a tip," said Susan. "Were they together the whole time, in this room?"

"Every morning that I delivered breakfast they were."

"Did she go to the convention events as well?"

"I'm not sure. One day I know she went to our spa. She was upset that breakfast was delivered late. Said she had a massage scheduled."

You didn't hear a name by any chance, did you?"

"No, sorry. Wait a minute. Susie or Cindy...Sandy. He called her Sandy."

"Thank you. You've been a real prince." Susan pulled a twenty out of her purse. "Take this for your troubles."

Valerie said, "What floor is the spa on?"

"Second floor. First right when you get out of the elevator."

Susan led Valerie down to the spa and marched up to the spa's main desk.

"Excuse me. Do you have a brochure?"

The woman with the tight black bun pointed to a plastic display rack on the counter.

Susan cleared her throat. "One of our coworkers is getting married and I'm the matron of honor so you know what that means."

The woman looked up from the computer screen and slipped on the glasses from the beaded chain around her neck. "And?"

"I've got to plan the bachelorette party. I thought a nice spa day, dinner, and then maybe get some of those Chippendale dancers to show up at the bar."

"We have bridal packages on page two."

"She stayed here last week and bragged to no end about her massage therapist. Said it was the best massage of her life. Can you look it up for us?"

She looked annoyed.

Susan said, "It's a huge bridal party, if you can accommodate us, that is."

The receptionist twisted her mouth into a stiff smile. "What's her name?"

Susan responded, "Sandy. It would have been middle of last week. Blond, young..."

The woman said, "Oh, Sandy Townshend. She has a standing appointment with Felix on Wednesdays."

"So she's local?" *Not what I expected.*

"No, she flies in from Hong Kong every week just to get a massage from our spa."

She didn't need to be sarcastic. I'll have to fill out one of those customer surveys and mention it. "Does Felix happen to be here now?" asked Susan.

"He's in the middle of a service. I'll pencil your party in. What date and time would you like?"

"I'll get you a count and call back for the reservations." She grabbed a business card. "He works every day?"

"10-4. Except for Mondays."

Once outside, Valerie said, "We should come back tomorrow."

"Today is Tuesday. Sandy headed to the spa after breakfast the day she was with Harold, right?" said Susan.

"Poor Madison had no idea. What was Harold's game? Standing affair, or a fling? Madison is a beautiful, young wife. Why did he feel the need to cheat on her?"

"I wonder how often Harold visited St. Louis?" said Susan.

Valerie followed Susan down the stairs to the lobby. "So we go home and pack?"

"And come back tomorrow morning."

Chapter 18

Susan had dinner with Evan, Cara, and Cara's parents. She'd met them at the Match Day Ceremony and again at graduation. She liked them well enough, but felt a little intimidated by them—not a feeling she was used to. They were both prominent doctors and here she was a retired teacher and Mike worked in the city permits office. Afterwards, she was exhausted and happy to curl up on Valerie's sofa bed.

The next morning, she and Valerie ate breakfast at the hotel coffee shop where they had a bird's eye view of everyone entering the hotel.

Valerie sipped her coffee and took a bite of her chocolate chip muffin. "So how was it last night? Where did you eat?"

"Charlie Gitto's on the hill. Fried ravioli. And butter cake."

"My favorite for special occasions. Maybe you can have the rehearsal dinner there. You and Mike have to plan it you know."

"That's a possibility. They all like Italian food, but who doesn't?"

"Hey, see the blond with the Gucci purse? Think that's her?"

"She's not stopping at the front desk."

Valerie gulped the rest of her coffee. "Let's hurry. I think she's going up the steps. Yep. She has to be heading to the spa."

"What are we supposed to say to her? Ask if she had an affair with Harold Chambers?"

"I have an idea. Try to look official. Follow my lead." She pulled a notebook out of her purse.

They stopped Sandy just as she was about to enter the spa. Susan said, "Excuse me, ma'am, are you Sandy Townshend?"

"Yes, why?"

"Can we speak to you for a moment?"

"I have an appointment."

"It will just take a moment." She led her away from the doorway and kept her voice low. "We understand you've had recent contact with a Mr. Harold Chambers."

"Contact? Are you a private investigator? Did his daughter have you follow me?"

"His daughter?"

"Yeah. Wouldn't leave him alone. Constant phone calls. Even showed up in town. Tell her to mind her own business."

"Alissa Chambers?"

"No, that wasn't it. Jada, Jenna, no, Janalyn. That was it."

Susan felt thoughts darting around in her head but grabbed her focus. "Was Mr. Chambers being harassed?"

"She claimed to be his daughter but he denied it. Said she was just after his money. I have a message for you to deliver. Tell her to back off. I had a fling and it's over now. I'm not involved and she should save her money."

"Where did you meet Mr. Chambers?"

"I come here for a massage appointment every Wednesday. Sometimes I get here early and grab a cup of coffee. He was here for some convention and the coffee shop was packed so he asked if he could sit down next to me. We started talking and one thing led to another. It was never meant to be anything more than a little fun."

Susan said, "Why would Janalyn hire a private investigator if she already knew how to contact her father?"

"I don't know why she thinks I'd have any influence over him. She hired *you* to convince *me* to convince *him* to talk her, right? Tell her to go back to Chicago and leave me out of this. Now, I have to go inside or I'll miss my appointment." She hustled through the spa door.

Susan said, "Did you get all that? Tell me I'm not getting senile."

Valerie said, "You're not. How did you know she'd assume you were a private investigator?"

"I didn't. I was going to say we were from the health department and were advising her to see her doctor because Harold Chambers had an STD."

Valerie laughed. "You can save that one for another time."

"Sandy said Janalyn should 'go back to Chicago.' How far is Chicago?"

"Five hours or so by car. You're not thinking of going out there, are you? We don't even have a last name."

"I'm going to have a chat with Madison and see if she knows anything about this 'daughter.' Let's go back to your place."

When they got to the apartment, Susan plopped down on the sofa and made a call. Madison sounded out of breath when she picked up.

"Madison, are you okay? "

"Yeah. I'm playing tennis. Trying to get out my frustration. I thought we had Harold's killer, and then Coach Cullins turns up dead. It happened right here at the club, you know. This is where we were supposed to meet and he didn't show up."

"How did he die? Lynette never said."

"He was stabbed in the locker room. I can't believe no one saw it happen. Lynette said the courts were closing and whoever was on the grounds would have been at the clubhouse."

"Did they find the murder weapon?"

"I don't think so."

"You were supposed to meet that night. It was before the press conference was scheduled to happen."

"And he was a no show. What if I'd gotten caught in the middle of it? Or, it could have been me they were after!"

"I think whatever Coach Cullins was going to announce was the reason he was killed. And I have another piece of information to ask you about."

"Go ahead."

"Did Harold have another daughter, besides Alissa?"

"No, why?"

"Ever heard Harold mention someone named Janalyn? I'm here in St. Louis and someone who was with Harold claims this Janalyn was harassing him and trying to get him to admit she was his daughter."

"Seriously? I never heard the name. And who was with Harold in St. Louis?"

"It's not important."

"It was another woman, right? I had a feeling something was up. He'd been so secretive lately. He was having an affair, wasn't he?"

Susan felt herself flush. She'd been working so hard on not sticking her foot in her mouth and here she went and did just that. "Not an affair. Just a one-night stand. She said it didn't mean anything. And you're so much prettier."

"I'm wondering what else he didn't tell me."

"Do you happen to have his cell phone, or did the police take it?"

"I've got it. Why?"

"We have a lead that Janalyn may live in Chicago. Can you access his call history so we can possibly track her down? I think they met here in St. Louis and if so, she could have planted the poisoned Snacky Sax here, before he got back on the plane. We may have been looking at this from the wrong angle."

"Then who killed Coach Cullins? Are you saying she flew here to Westbrook and killed him? What's the motive?"

"We're working on it. Call me back if you get into his phone and see any numbers from the Chicago area."

"Will do. Thanks, Susan."

Valerie said, "Did I hear you say Coach Cullins was stabbed?"

"Yeah. And Madison was in the dark about Janalyn. She's going to get back to us. How about we do some packing in the meantime."

"If I get everything together, maybe I can go back to Westbrook with you—before Jazzy and Elijah. I can pack a few boxes of essentials and have the rest boxed and labeled for when the moving truck comes. Once Elijah's in the house, it won't be so easy to unpack and organize."

"Okay, then let's get to it. Where do you want me to start?"

"How about in the kitchen. Wrap up the dishes and pots and pans. I'll go through the linen closet and start on my bedroom."

They worked for hours before realizing it was past lunch time. Susan felt her blood sugar dropping. "Is it okay if we grab a bite to eat?"

"Of course." She walked into the kitchen and opened the cabinets. "I can't believe you got all this packed so quickly."

"I'm pretty good when it comes to organizing. What are you in the mood for?"

"There's a nice Vietnamese place not far from here. Pho Grand. It looks like an old house from the outside. Jenny's ice cream is practically around the corner for dessert, I'm just saying."

"I'll get my purse."

Chapter 19

The next morning, Susan woke to the sound of her phone vibrating on the coffee table next to the sofa bed. She reached for her glasses and looked at the screen.

"Madison?"

"Hey, guess what? I got into Harold's phone. He used the same pin for everything. Anyhow, I saw a Chicago number. It looks like this person was rather persistent. Eleven calls. The last call was made the day he left St. Louis to come home."

"Excellent. Let me get something to write with." She grabbed her purse and pulled out the notebook she carried around with her. "I'm ready." She copied down the number.

"Do you think this so called daughter of his killed him?"

"I don't know. If she felt she was entitled to a share of the company and Harold refused to recognize her as his daughter, I can see how she'd have a motive."

"But what about Coach Cullins? She'd have to have flown to New York last week. And what was her motive there?"

"I don't know. Maybe she suspected he was the silent partner. She hoped to convince him she had a right to a stake in the company and he refused. I'm surprised she hasn't approached you."

"Perhaps she didn't want to come forward as his daughter or she didn't realize I'd be inheriting part of the company. Did she even know he died?"

"I'll try to get some answers. I'll talk to you after I talk to Janalyn."

"Good luck. And thanks for doing this. I have nightmares every night about the murder. I don't think I'll be able to sleep until someone is behind bars."

After she put down the phone, Valerie walked in. "Was that Mike?"

"No. Madison called back with Janalyn's phone number and I've got it right here." She waved her notebook. "Let's give it a whirl."

"Hang on. What are you going to say? We think you killed Harold Chambers?"

"We could pretend to be lawyers and say we need to see her about her inheritance. That would get her attention."

"Boy, you sure can lie like a rug. I think we should think this through. Maybe do a little investigating before we talk to her. Besides, it's early. She may still be asleep."

"Madison was up."

"It's an hour later in New York. Don't forget we're on central time."

"Do you think Jazzy will help us?"

"She'll say to mind our own business. But…there's someone I think will help us. He was a friend of my husband. He liked my blueberry muffins. Anyway, he worked in Jazzy's precinct, then retired and started a small bond chaser business. He might help us with a background check."

"Do you have his number?"

"I'm sure I do."

"What are you waiting for?"

"Again, it's early. I'll make us some breakfast, then we'll call."

Valerie whipped up a batch of French toast. "I got this recipe from *The Lazy Vegetarian*. It uses vanilla almond milk in the batter. Gives it some sweetness."

"It's delicious. I'll make this for Mike."

"I have a feeling he's going to be suspicious of your cooking since the beet chili."

When they finished eating, Valerie checked the kitchen clock and grabbed her phone, scrolled through her contacts, and connected with her old friend.

"Jerry? It's Valerie. Yeah, it's been a while. I'm fine. Actually getting ready to move to upstate New York. Jazzy got a new job so we're all going together."

"That's wonderful. A new start. What can I do for you?" replied the voice on the phone.

"It's kind of a long story. A man I sat next to on a flight died right beside me. We found out he had been poisoned."

"Poisoned? Are you okay?"

"I'm fine. The poor widow is beside herself. I know how that feels, losing your hubby. The detective, my friend's daughter, has her hands full and we are helping out. Unofficially, of course. Anyway, we have a lead. If I text you a phone number and a first name, can you find the last name and do a background check?"

"Business is a little slow here. Of course I can. I'll get back to you later today."

"Thanks. You're a gem."

Susan said, "Sounds like he's willing to help."

"Yeah. Why don't we do some packing in the meantime."

Susan packed up the bookshelves and knick-knacks while Valerie zipped through the bathroom and finished the closets. By mid-afternoon, the living room was full of packed boxes and bags of Goodwill donations were lined up by the door like soldiers in a mess line.

"I'd say we made a lot of progress," said Susan.

"We sure have. Not too much more to do."

Valerie's phone rang. "It's Jerry."

"Valerie, I got the info you wanted. The girl's name is Janalyn Reynolds. She's on the dean's list at Northwestern, biology major, and lives in an apartment just off campus. No criminal history. She doesn't have a driver's license registered in this state. Born in Evansville. Mother is listed as Candace Reynolds. No father listed on the birth certificate."

"You're a gem. Can you text me her address?"

"Consider it done. Best of luck with your move."

"Thanks, Jerry."

When she finished, she shared the info with Susan.

"Well, what are we waiting for? Let's make the call."

"What are we going to say?"

"What she wants to hear. Where's the number?"

"Don't go scaring her off. Think it through, first."

"Shh." She punched in the number. One ring, two rings, three... "Hello, I'm looking for a Janalyn Reynolds."

"That's me. Who is this?"

"I'm trying to contact the daughter of Harold Chambers. Is this she?"

"Yes. Finally. Yes, I'm his daughter."

"I have good news and bad news. I'm not sure if you were informed that your father is recently deceased."

"Deceased? As in dead? Oh, no. I just spoke to him last week. What happened?"

"He was," she cleared her throat, "murdered." She listened for a reaction. Janalyn was silent on the other end. "Did you hear me?"

"Yes. It's just, I'm in shock. What happened?"

"The police are investigating."

"So where's the good news? You said good news and bad news."

"The good news is, he left you a share of his company. Of course, you'll have to verify you are his daughter. His daughter is unaware of other siblings and is planning on challenging it."

"I recently found out his identity. He refused to acknowledge me."

"Why was it a secret?"

"My mother never wanted a hand out. She's a successful professor at Northwestern. Always proud."

"Were they married?"

"No. He worked in the admissions office and she taught. They were together a few months, then she realized he'd been cheating on her the whole time. When she told him she was pregnant, he refused to believe it...I...was his. She said he was a no-good scum bag. Didn't want me to have anything to do with him."

"But she wound up telling you."

"She's got terminal cancer. She thought I should know."

"I'm so sorry."

"He owes her something. He owes me something. The medical bills have wiped out every penny she's got and I'm still a student. He's rich. He could at least have offered to throw a few crumbs our way. Mom needs to know I'll be okay."

"Do you have any idea who might have had him in his crosshairs? He was murdered. Poisoned."

"Poisoned?"

"Cyanide."

"I'm sure he deserved it. I don't know. He was together with some bimbo at a hotel in St. Louis last week. Grainy voice. Sounded old. I got the feeling she wasn't his wife. If I were his wife and found out he was sleeping with someone else, I'd be mad."

"Mad enough to kill? What about if you were his daughter and he didn't acknowledge you?"

"I hope you don't think I had anything to do with this. Who are you again?"

"I didn't mean to push like that. I know the wife and she's very distraught. I'm trying to help her get some answers. And she wants you to have what you deserve. We said we'd try to locate you. Can we meet?"

"I live in Evanston. Are you in New York?"

"Visiting a friend in St. Louis. Are you available?"

"It's a long drive. I can't get out there. But, I can grab a bus and meet you halfway. There's a diner where the bus stops for a dinner break. I'll talk to you if you're willing to meet there."

Susan looked at her watch and covered the phone. Valerie nodded when she asked if it was feasible. "Sure. If we leave now, we can meet you for dinner. See you then."

"Don't you need the address?"

"Um, yes. Of course we do. Text it to my number. See you soon."

Valerie said, "Why was she so free with her life story? She doesn't know you. That's strange."

"Sounded like all of that emotion has been bottled up for a long time and finally someone was willing to listen."

"What are we hoping to gain by seeing her? She all but admitted she tried to contact him and came to St. Louis."

"Let's see if she ever came to New York. Your friend said she was a biology major. Fertilizer? Chemical know how? And did she meet Harold face to face? Did she have an opportunity to slip him the poisoned Snacky Sax?"

"You want me to call him back?"

"See if he can find out if she was in Westbrook before Harold died, or around the time Cullins was murdered."

Valerie nodded and took her phone into the other room, smoothing her hair along the way as if she was doing Facetime.

Does she like Jerry as more than a friend? She called Lynette.

"Lynette, how are the girls?"

"They're fine. How's the packing going?'

"I'd say Valerie is close to done. She's thinking she might even fly back with me and start settling in before Jazmin comes. She already has the bed in the new place and she's packed a box of kitchen items and bathroom necessities."

"Jazmin is hoping to move up her start date. I'm swamped."

"I heard you found the murder weapon. Mark Cullins was stabbed, right?"

"We don't have the murder weapon, but yes, he was stabbed. How did you know? We didn't release that detail."

"Madison. She was supposed to meet with Cullins at the tennis club. Now she knows why he didn't show up. No one saw what happened? No security footage?"

"No cameras are allowed in the locker rooms and people came in and out of the club all day long. The killer had to have planned ahead and snuck the knife into the locker room with him."

"How about finger prints?"

"Do you know how many men wander in and out of that locker room? Yeah, there are tons of prints, but nothing to help us find the killer."

"Lynette, we found out Harold had another daughter who lives in Chicago. Harold refused to acknowledge her and this daughter needed a share of his money. Her mother is dying of cancer and the girl is a college student. And don't ask. We were chatting with someone and it just came up."

"Just came up. Okay. So what's the girl's name?"

"Janalyn Reynolds. She's a student at Northwestern."

"And I'm sure you already spoke to her, right?"

"Yes, and we're going to meet with her tonight."

"Seriously? You think this girl is a killer but you're going to meet with her. Will you ever learn?"

"I'm not doing anything stupid. We're meeting in public at a diner. We'll be fine. Can you check and see if Janalyn Reynolds was in Westbrook recently? It's Janalyn, J-A-N…"

"I can spell. I'll get right on it. When I'm done catching the bank robbers who are at large. And after I stop the rash of attempted break-ins which are likely related."

"Break-ins? In our neighborhood? Or yours? Or Jonathan's?"

"No, but someone reported suspicious activity in the neighborhood where Jazmin and Valerie bought the house. We've got extra patrols in the area."

"Why do you think the break-ins are related to the robberies?"

"A similar van was spotted at both banks and one of the attempted break-ins."

"You'll tell the patrols to pay extra attention to Valerie's place, right? It's sitting empty. Good thing she may be flying home soon." Then she wondered if Valerie would be a sitting duck. Maybe coming back to an empty house wasn't such a good idea.

"Mia's crying, I've got to go. Be careful. See you in a few days."

Valerie came in from the bedroom. "Jerry called me back. Janalyn Reynolds bought a round trip ticket to New York the week before Harold was murdered."

"She came to Westbrook?"

"Twice. He traced a hotel reservation to the Holiday Inn. Two reservations. One a month ago, and the other a few days ago."

"When Cullins was killed."

"This trip may prove very enlightening. Are you ready to go?"

Chapter 20

"How close are we?" asked Susan. Rain pelted the windshield and the headlight glare off the road made her eyes ache. She reached for a handful of Kettle Corn they'd picked up in anticipation of the road trip.

Valerie grasped the steering wheel and glued her eyes to the slick road. "Almost there. What are we going to do if she confesses? I mean, I doubt she will, but even if she does, she's not gonna to sit and wait for us to call the police. I'm not sure pushing her is a good idea anymore."

"We won't go that far. Let's see what she says, and if we're convinced she's a plausible suspect, we'll let Jazmin and Lynette follow up." Susan took a swig of Diet Coke and offered the bag of Kettle Corn to Valerie, who grabbed a handful.

"I almost feel sorry for her. Her mother dying of cancer and all," said Valerie.

"We don't even know if that's the truth. Why did she come to Westbrook, and then come after Harold again in St. Louis? She obviously didn't get the answer she wanted from Harold the first time."

Valerie said, "And how do we know she's really his daughter? Her mother told her...or didn't. Maybe she *thinks* she put it all together. We have no idea what her mother actually said."

"True. Though what a terrible thing to lie about your mother having cancer. I think she was telling the truth. Her voice broke when she was telling me—like she was about to cry." Susan couldn't imagine lying about your mother dying.

"How did she find out about Coach Cullins? What gave her the idea he was the secret partner?" asked Valerie.

"Internet research or a private investigator. Maybe she did more than meet with Harold. Maybe she followed him and overhead them talking. Or snooped around at Succex like we did."

"That secretary at Succex sure has got loose lips."

"And one more thing. Why was Harold unwilling to acknowledge her if it was true.?"

"Hopefully, we'll have answers soon."

Valerie took the next exit and pulled into a rest stop housing a trailer-like diner. "I don't see any buses here."

"We have a few minutes. Let's go in. Do you have any umbrellas?"

"In the back seat." Valerie pulled in front of the diner. "Come on while the rain is letting up."

After running into the diner, they shook the water from their umbrellas and followed the hostess past an old fashioned cash register perched on a glass case full of assorted pies. Their wet shoes squeaked on the linoleum as they walked to a booth near the window. Twangy music emanated from a jukebox. Susan hated country music and wished they'd turn it down. She and Valerie both ordered coffee and waited. And waited some more.

Valerie looked at her watch. "She's late."

Susan said, "I think I see bus headlights. Wait. No."

"How about there?" said Valerie.

"It's a minivan, not a bus." Susan sipped her now tepid coffee.

"There's a bus turning into the rest stop now. That has to be it," said Valerie.

"You're right." Susan craned her neck and squinted but the rain had picked up and it was difficult to see who was exiting the bus. First, an elderly couple with a young boy came in. Susan assumed it was a grandson. Then, a girl with a raincoat hood pulled over her head, wearing a backpack.

"I'll bet that's her," said Susan. She waved, but the girl walked past and sat down.

"How about her?" Valerie pointed to a young lady, then noticed she was holding the hand of a toddler. "I guess not."

"I hope she didn't back out."

"There's someone else. Wait."

"It can't be her. She's waving one of those white sticks. She must be blind. She's asking the hostess something. She's coming toward us."

The woman stopped in front of their booth. "Susan Wiles?"

Susan felt flustered. "How…I didn't realize…"

"That I'm visually impaired? Not the first thing I announce over the phone, but I recognized your voice."

Susan said loudly, "Sit down. I'm sorry we made you come all the way here on a bus. If we'd known…"

"I'm used to public transportation. I get along very well without a car." She waved her hand and the waitress, who seemed to know her, came over with a pot of coffee. "And I'm blind, not deaf. No need to shout."

Valerie said, "Don't blind people wear sunglasses?"

"What for?" asked Janalyn, as if the question was absurd.

"You know, to protect your eyes."

"Do deaf people wear earmuffs?"

Susan tried to alleviate the awkwardness of the moment. "Let's order dinner. My treat." She tried to hand Janalyn a menu, then corrected herself and pulled it away.

The waitress came by. Janalyn ordered a burger; Susan and Valerie did the same.

Susan felt guilt crawling over her like fire ants. "I'm sorry, I wasn't entirely truthful on the phone."

"What do you mean?" asked Janalyn.

"I don't know if Harold Chambers left you anything or if he ever acknowledged you as his daughter. I confess. We're snooping around to find murder suspects."

Valerie added, "We thought we'd nailed the killer, but then he went and got murdered."

"And you thought I killed the man I was working so hard to have a relationship with?"

"Um, yes. I'm so sorry."

"And now that you see I'm blind, I'm no longer a suspect?"

"Well, you'd have needed to see to switch out his Snacky Sax. And the second victim was stabbed."

"I can stab as well as anyone. I use my cane, I follow the sound and... Bam."

Susan and Valerie jumped.

"I can hit a mosquito with an arrow a football field away. You'd be surprised."

Susan leaned in. "Really?" She'd grossly underestimated what blind people could do.

Valerie waved her hand in front of Janalyn's face. "Not to be politically incorrect or anything, but I don't believe you can hit a fly with an arrow."

"A mosquito. Not a fly. And, you're right. Of course, I can't. And I can't measure out poison, let alone handle it without possibly poisoning myself. And stab someone? Really?"

Susan exhaled. "For a minute, you had me going."

The waitress set their food on the table. Susan poured ketchup on her fries. "How did you manage to fly to New York?"

"My mother made sure from an early age that I would be as independent as possible. That's why she never dwelt on who my father was until she realized I might need a safety net."

"I'm sorry about your mother. Is there a chance…" Valerie didn't get to complete her question.

"No, I'm afraid not. But I don't want to go there." Janalyn's phone signaled a text had arrived.

Valerie reached for the phone. "Want me to read it to you?"

"It's my mother, and, no. I can read and write my own texts. I'll answer later."

Susan sipped her warmed up coffee. "When you first met Harold in New York, what was that like? Did you go to his home?"

"I met him at his office at Succex. I'd called first but saved the big reveal until then."

"And how did he react?" asked Susan.

"He denied it. Then he asked questions about my mother, like he was believing me. Then…"

"Then what?"

"He all of a sudden did a 180. Yelled at me to leave. Said I was just after his money, like everyone else."

"And nothing happened to cause the change?" asked Valerie.

"I think someone was listening outside the door. I could swear I heard footsteps. I hadn't shut the door all the way. He told me to leave and when I went out, I smelled perfume."

"Perfume?"

"Or else someone was carrying a floral arrangement. It smelled like fresh flowers. Carnations, maybe."

"And this person didn't say anything?" asked Susan.

"No."

"Are you sure it was a woman?" asked Valerie.

"I said I smelled a floral scent. I assumed it was a woman."

After a brief pause, Susan broke the silence. "But it could have been a man holding flowers? I mean, when we went to Succex, the secretary had a big vase full of fresh flowers on her desk."

"You figure it out."

"When you saw him, I mean when you *met* with him in St. Louis, was he still in denial?"

"Yes. I mean, he was nicer when I first arrived, then he got a phone call. He tried to whisper but we were in a hotel room and my hearing is very good. He said something about it was going to be all right and they would be gone by then."

"Did you hear anything else? A name? Did he sound like he was talking to a business partner or someone like a friend?" asked Valerie.

"I don't know. He was trying to calm the person down. Be reassuring. That's all I got."

Susan said, "We know you went back to New York a second time. After Harold was dead."

"I didn't know he was dead. I wanted to try one more time to convince him. When I got to town, I heard on the local news he was dead. I knew he hadn't acknowledged me at that point. My next move was to go home, get a lawyer, and try to prove paternity and contest the will."

"Did you cross paths with Mark Cullins?" asked Susan.

"Who?"

Valerie clarified. "We think he was Harold's silent partner. Did you approach him hoping to get a share of the business?"

"No, of course not. That doesn't even make sense. His business partner wasn't about to share the company with his dead partner's secret daughter. Frankly, I didn't know he had a business partner." She picked up her phone. "I have to catch the return bus. It'll be stopping any time now."

Susan said, "Don't forget your stick."

Janalyn sighed. "It's a cane, not a stick. Do you mind if I put on my raincoat first?"

Valerie said, "Thank you for meeting with us."

Susan pulled a business card out of her purse and tucked it in Janalyn's hand. "My father is a retired attorney. I'll ask him if he knows anyone who may be able to help you get what you deserve. And I'm sorry about your mother."

"Me too." She grabbed her cane and went out into the rain. A bus pulled up minutes later.

Valerie said, "I don't think she's our killer."

"No, but did you hear what she said about the floral scent?"

"Could have been anything. Maybe the secretary trying not to interrupt, or even a student."

"Or someone who worked in a nursery?"

Valerie sighed. "We're back thinking Carmine Vitulli?"

"We never really ruled him out."

"What about the call in the hotel room? I'll bet Harold was talking to Cullins."

"Janalyn smelled perfume. Thinks it was a woman."

"The secretary had fresh flowers on her desk. Carmine grows carnations at his nursery. I say as soon as we get back to Westbrook, we make another visit to Succex and reevaluate our suspicions about Carmine Vitulli."

Chapter 21

Mike was waiting at the gate when Susan and Valerie's flight arrived. Valerie had managed to get everything packed and with the threat of break-ins in her new neighborhood, she didn't want to leave her new house vacant.

Mike said, "That's all you've got? Two big boxes and a couple of suitcases?"

"The rest is coming on the moving truck. Jazzy and Elijah will be arriving sooner than we thought."

"That's great. Lynette will be grateful for the help."

Susan said, "Lynette said there's been a series of attempted break-ins. Does she think they're related to the bank robberies?"

"I don't know. Why would they be? I mean, the bank robbers already have the moula from the bank," said Mike.

"As soon as we can afford it, Jazzy promised we'd get a security system installed at the new house. I can't wait to see it again."

"We should be there before dark." He pulled the luggage cart into an elevator that led to the parking garage. "Do you want to stop at a grocery store or anything?"

"Yes, if it's not too much trouble. I sold my car to one of Jazzy's friends in St. Louis. First thing tomorrow I'm going to see about replacing it."

Traffic was lighter than expected. After hitting the grocery store, Susan and Mike helped bring the groceries and Valerie's luggage inside.

Susan put the milk and eggs into the fridge. "Do you want us to bring over a card table and a folding chair so you have a place to eat?"

"I'll be all right. It's just for a few days."

Mike said, "Let us know if you change your mind."

After they left, Valerie wished she had her dresser so she could put away the clothes she had with her. Instead, she unpacked a few of the essential kitchen items. She'd have to remember to pick up a step stool so she could store the pots above the stove.

Back in St. Louis, she'd stored her baking sheets in the drawer under the stove. She tugged on the drawer but found it hard to pull open. *It was perfectly smooth when we did the walk through, wasn't it? Wait, I was about to try it, then got distracted.* She stuck her hand in behind the drawer and after a tough round of tug of war, pulled out a small accordion recipe file with a few recipe cards inside. She kept her coupons in a similar holder. *It must have fallen off the counter at some point.*

Grandma's chicken pot pie…Great Grammy's chili, Mom's Sour Cream Bundt Cake…These look like family recipes. I'll bet Mrs. Russell will be upset when she discovers she left them behind. She thought about mailing them to her, but when she checked the paperwork for the mortgage, she couldn't find a forwarding address.

After making herself a sandwich and a can of soup for dinner, Valerie took a long, hot shower and stretched out on her bed to watch Netflix on her laptop. She must have dozed off but a noise outside jarred her awake. She ran inside to the dining area, turned on the backyard lights, though it wasn't quite dark yet, and peeked out the sliding glass doors. Nothing. It was perfectly quiet. She'd feel better when they installed a security system. Living in an apartment in the city after her hubby died never made her feel unsafe. Now, in a middle class housing development in a university town she felt scared.

She settled back in her room, then heard knocking on the front door. *Maybe Susan is stopping by with the folding table after all. That must be what I heard before.* She traded her robe for a pair of pull-on shorts and a t-shirt. The knocking was insistent by this point.

"I'm coming. Who the heck comes knocking at night? Hold your horses!" She checked the peep hole, then unlocked the door.

The backyard neighbor stood at the door with a plate of cookies. "I saw you'd moved in and wanted to bring you these to welcome you to the neighborhood."

She hoped the neighbor hadn't heard her ranting through the door. "That's so sweet. Come on in." She put the cookies on the counter. "If you told me your name, I'm afraid my senility is showing."

"It's Clara and when you get to be our age the brain starts going," she laughed.

"Well, I'm Valerie. I can make us coffee. If I can find the coffee maker."

"No worries. Just checking if you need anything. Hubby and I are about to watch *Jeopardy*."

Valerie picked up the recipe file. "I found this stuck in the stove drawer. It looks like it contains family recipes. Do you have any idea where the Russells went? They didn't leave a forwarding address."

"Better question is why they went so suddenly, like I said before. Then again, with Chuck's recent behavior, who knows?"

"What do you mean?"

"He was always friendly. And he'd let Brock out to play on the swings without him all the time. It's completely fenced in, as you saw. A few weeks ago, Brock was outside and Chuck came running out followed by April, that's his wife. He started screaming at her about not letting Brock go out unattended. It was weird, and I heard her ask him why not, but he told her to trust him. Trust him? I think he owed her an explanation, don't you?"

"Maybe work was making him tense. What did he do for a living?"

"He managed a bank not far from here." She lowered her voice to a whisper. "The one that was robbed."

"I heard there were two bank robberies. Wasn't one over by city hall?"

"Yes, you're right. It was a different bank altogether. I'd say the robberies put him on edge except he started acting strange before that."

"Strange, how?"

"He used to be outside fussing with the lawn or pulling weeds after work. April said it relaxed him. But about a month or so ago, he stopped. In fact, the grass was getting so long I was worried maybe he'd gotten hurt. April mowed it herself one day while he was at work. She was worried about him. She confided in me that he'd become short tempered with both her and Brock."

"Did she say why they decided to leave in such a hurry?"

"She said Chuck wanted a new start and he had some idea about opening a business but didn't say what kind of business. April didn't want to leave. She loved the house and picked the neighborhood specifically for the great schools. Brock was going to start first grade. She loved his kindergarten teacher."

"She didn't give any hints about why or where they were going?"

"None. I'm not even sure she knew herself. Well, I'd better get going. If you need anything, come over."

"Thanks."

After Clara left, Valerie Googled April and Charles Russell. *I suppose Chuck is short for Charles but who knows? It could even be his middle name.* A slew of people named Russell popped up—too many to possibly dig through. It was hard for her to put her curiosity to rest. She Googled the robbery. "Three tellers and two customers were told to lie on the ground. Charles Russell, bank manager, was held at gunpoint and forced to open the safe. Two masked robbers were in and out within minutes. No one was injured."

She searched for information on the other robbery—the one across from city hall. "Two masked robbers barged into the bank mid-morning...shouted at the customers and teller to hit the ground. Forced the bank manager to open the safe. No one was injured. The robbers haven't been caught but area banks are stepping up security." *Sounds awfully similar. Has to be the same robbers. Chuck Russell felt unsafe letting his child into the fenced yard. Sounds like it started before the bank was robbed. And what about the man Clara saw in the backyard?*

Chapter 22

Luckily, Susan had a schedule, or lack of one, that allowed her to play chauffeur. She picked up Valerie and they hit the auto showrooms early. Valerie knew what she wanted—the same reliable car she'd sold back in St. Louis. Before lunch, Valerie drove off the lot in her brand new, ruby red, Ford Escape.

"That's the fastest car deal I've ever witnessed," said Susan.

"Sporty, ain't it?" said Valerie. "And I can start it from inside the house with the app."

"It'd take me a while to get used to not using a key, but getting the air conditioning going before getting in during the summer months? How cool is that?" She hadn't intended the pun but found it amusing.

"Let's drop off your car and ride together," said Valerie. "I'll follow you."

Valerie's fingers fumbled across the dashboard in an effort to turn on some music. Proud of starting her car from the app, now she couldn't find the radio switch! Never mind syncing the music from her phone to the car like the dealer suggested. By the time she pulled into Susan's driveway, she'd given up.

Susan slid into the passenger seat and took a deep breath. "Ahh, the new car smell."

"New car aroma sounds better." Valerie adjusted the new sunglasses she'd picked up at the mall and said, "Where to? Succex, or celebratory lunch?"

"How about Succex and then lunch." Susan pulled down the visor with the lighted mirror and ran her fingers over the back-up camera. "Maybe it's time to trade in my Prius." *Be real. You don't have the money, especially since Mike is considering retirement.* "Why don't you turn on some music?"

Valerie didn't answer. When they got to Succex, she parked across two spaces.

"I thought you hated when people hogged more than one spot?"

"That's before I had my new baby. Come on. I've got to remember to take the key with me when I go inside."

Inside, the secretary was busy filing papers. Susan moved as close as she could to her without seeming weird, and took a sniff. *No hint of floral perfume*

The secretary remembered them from the last time. "Morning, ladies. Are you back to enroll your grandson?"

"He gets into town later this week. I had a few more questions," said Valerie. "Can you tell me more about the faculty make-up?"

"We have a diverse staff." She quickly added, "Old, young, male, female…all different backgrounds."

"Elijah works well with female tutors. We had a man once and they spent the whole hour talking sports."

"We have two females on staff. Edna Marquette, and Jaira Campbell."

"Tell me more," said Valerie.

"Edna retired from teaching public school. She has forty years of experience under her belt. Jaira came to us fresh off a master's degree with no teaching experience, but she's got a way of relating to these kids. She was a math major and has done wonders getting these kids up to snuff for the math portion of the SAT."

"Is she here today?"

"She is. She's expecting a client in a few minutes but you can pop in and meet her. Her office is around the corner."

Valerie led the way and they found Jaira at her computer.

"Can I help you?"

Valerie explained the situation. "Elijah is a workaholic. Anything you teach him, he'll soak up like a sponge."

"I'm looking forward to meeting him. Any questions? I've got a client in a few minutes."

Valerie walked around the desk, pretending to inspect the book shelf, sniffing for perfume.

Susan said, "It's too bad about Mr. Chambers. Must be hard on the faculty and students losing their leader that way."

"I know. I hear the funeral was packed. I was out of town the past two weeks and missed it."

"Must have been surprised coming back to the news." said Susan.

"My colleagues had contacted me. I'm glad it wasn't a complete shock."

Valerie extended her hand. "We'll be seeing you soon."

Outside, Valerie said, "I did smell perfume but not floral. Something woodsy."

"And she was out of town when the murder happened."

"I doubt the one with forty-years of experience was involved in this mess." Valerie started her car with her phone.

Susan said, "Yeah. It was a vague clue. Could have been anyone, not necessarily a faculty member."

"Do you mind if we stop at the bank? I have to set up an account. There's a bank in my neighborhood."

"The one that was robbed? You sure that's where you want to start an account?"

Valerie said, "It's like flying a plane after there's been an accident. You can bet security's going to be extra vigilant."

They drove over to the bank. Once inside, Valerie waited for customer service.

"Ms. Holmes? Come on over. What can I do for you today?"

"I just moved to town and need to set up a checking and savings account."

"We're happy to serve you. Go ahead and fill out this form while I copy your driver's license."

Valerie grabbed a pen from the mesh cup on the desk. "I heard there was a robbery here not too long ago."

"Yes. Very scary."

"You were here when it happened?"

"Yes. Forced to lie on the floor; terrified of being shot. Never prayed so hard in my life."

"And they haven't caught the robbers?"

"No. I'd feel better if they did."

"I believe the person I bought the house from worked here. Chuck Russell."

"Yes, Mr. Russell. If it weren't for him, we might all be dead. One of the robbers held a gun to his head and had him open the safe. He did exactly as he was told, no heroics."

"And where did he move to?"

"No one knows. In fact, it came as a shock to all of us. A few days after the robbery, we show up to work and there's a new manager. Speculation is he was fired because of the robbery. Something about the silent alarm not being activated. None of us who worked with him believe it." She made a copy and handed the license back to Valerie. "And we heard his son was ill. I hope he moved somewhere with good medical care, like the one in Memphis. The one Marlo Thomas's actor daddy started. I loved her in *That Girl*."

"Danny Thomas. You mean St. Jude's."

"That's the one. I hear they don't charge the families."

"Hope it all works out for him." *Maybe that's why they left in a hurry. If their son was sick and St. Jude's had an opening...*

"If you'll enter a pin number on the pad, you won't have to come in again." She stretched the touch pad over the desk.

Valerie punched in her usual pin, Elijah's birthday "I heard there was a second robbery across town."

"Yes, we all heard about it. They tried to blame their manager, too. I know because my best friend used to be a teller here. She transferred when she moved into a new condo across town."

"So her manager is still there?"

"As of yesterday, anyway. I'm sure I'd have heard if Marie got a new boss."

Valerie gave back the signed forms and gathered her things. "So I'll be getting a card in the mail?"

"Yes, within a few days. The checks as well. Congratulations on your new house."

Back in the car, Susan said, "That's a coincidence, don't you think? Both bank managers were blamed for the robberies?"

"If you're a manager, it's your job to be sure everything runs smoothly. Security is part of it."

Susan said, "Weird, though. The robbers knew both of those banks had a lapse in security that would make it easy for them to rob."

"You think Chuck Russell knew the bank was going to be robbed?"

"He needed money for his sick kid, right? How hard would it have been to disarm the silent alarm? Maybe he was part of it."

"What about the manager across town?" asked Valerie.

"Hmmm. You have a new bank account, but maybe you need to inquire about some other financial matter. At the other bank."

"Like what? I'm going to China and need foreign currency? Nowadays you can put it all on a credit card, as long as you've got one with no fees. If that..."

Susan said, "Stop. Nothing so elaborate."

"What are you hoping to do? Question the bank manager about his part in the robbery? Lynette would kill you. Even I see where that's not our place."

"Maybe not question him, but have a chat."

"I wouldn't mind driving across town." Valerie started the car, keys in hand. "Let's go."

The bank across town wasn't crowded. Two security guards stood at the entrance.

"See," said Valerie. "Beefing up the security to reassure the customers." She nodded to the guards on her way inside.

"What do we do now?" asked Susan.

"Let's talk to one of the tellers." She walked right up to the counter and asked the teller about starting an account.

"You'll have to talk with customer service. Sign the list on the table by the sofa and they'll call you."

Valerie leaned over the counter and whispered. "I heard about the bank robbery. I'm a little uneasy about leaving my money here. Could I speak to the manager?"

The teller looked around. "Sure. He just came back from lunch. Go on over."

Valerie led the way. "Excuse me. You're the manager, right?"

"I am. How can I help you today?"

"I'm new to town and have to find a new home for my retirement savings. This is the closest bank to my new house, but I'm a little worried. I heard there was a robbery here recently."

"Yes, that's true. No one was injured and we've since increased our security. You have nothing to worry about."

"How did they get in? I heard it was in broad daylight. I see guards outside."

"There was a glitch in the alarm system. It failed to activate. One of the men forced me to open the safe; another forced everyone down on the floor. It was over quickly and, thank God, no one was hurt."

"Did they catch who did it?"

"No, not yet." He fidgeted, looking around the bank rather than directly at Valerie.

"You must be rattled after that."

"I was. I am. But the alarm system has been completely overhauled. I can assure you it won't happen again."

"I feel better now that I heard it from the horse's mouth," said Valerie. She smiled and walked out the door with Susan. They got settled in the car and were headed home when Susan's phone rang.

"Hello? Hello? I can't hear you. What?"

A barely audible whisper came through. "Call your daughter for me. Someone's in the house."

Chapter 23

"Hello. I can't hear you. Who is this?"

"It's Madison Chambers. I'm hiding in my bedroom closet. Someone's in here. Call the police for me. Call your daughter."

"Why didn't you call 911?"

"I don't want police barging into the street with sirens on. I'm afraid I'll be taken hostage. Hurry"

"Hang on. I'll get help." Susan immediately called Lynette, praying she'd answer. *One ring, two, three. God, don't let it go to voice mail.* She was about to hang up and call 911.

Lynette picked up on the fourth ring. "Mom?"

"Lynette, there's an emergency. Please hurry. Madison Chambers is hiding in her bedroom closet as we speak. There's an intruder in her house. Right now. No sirens."

Valerie said, "Oh, my God. What's going on?"

"You heard. Lynette's on the way. Let's swing by and make sure it turns out okay. Hurry! Let's see how fast this new baby can fly across town."

Valerie zipped through neighborhoods, past the university, and turned onto Madison's street. "This is dangerous. We can't go in if the police aren't there yet."

"Of course not." Susan knew herself well enough to realize she'd have to temper her 'enthusiasm.' Besides, she heard Lynette inside her head telling her not to be stupid and put herself in danger. It seemed as if Valerie already knew her pretty well. *What are we walking into?* Madison's house came into view. "That's Lynette's car parked in the driveway. Let's go."

Pulse racing, Susan ran to the partially open front door, out of breath, followed by Valerie. *What if we're too late? Why didn't Madison call 911 instead of wasting time calling me first?* She caught her breath when she saw Madison, alive in the living room.

"Susan? Valerie? You came. If it wasn't for you…"

"Thank God you're alive!" Instead of walking into a murder scene as she'd feared, she walked in on Lynette taking Madison's statement.

"Mom, we're in the middle of something. I'll call you later."

Susan ignored the gentle nudge and took a seat on the sofa.

Madison continued. "I was in the master bedroom. I have a standing tennis lesson every week but I woke up so depressed over missing Harold that I canceled. My car was in the garage so whoever it was didn't know anyone was in here."

Lynette said, "You said you have a standing appointment. Do you suspect the intruder is someone you know? Someone familiar with your schedule?"

"Who? I…no, it was a woman's voice. Spanish accent."

"So she spoke to you?"

"No. Not to me."

Lynette said, "Let's start at the beginning. It's okay. The officer checked every room in the house and the back yard. Whoever was here is gone now."

"I was in my bedroom, resting. Crying, really. I heard glass shattering."

Lynette continued writing. "Yes, we noticed the broken window."

"Then I heard someone in Harold's office. Sounded like furniture was being moved and I heard thumps. Then I...I..."

Lynette looked up. "It's okay. Take your time."

Valerie said, "I'll get you a glass of water."

Madison continued. "Then, I felt like my heart was going to beat through my chest. I heard the stairs creaking. Someone was coming upstairs! I panicked and ran into my closet to hide. I didn't know what else to do."

Susan said, "That was a smart move. You could have been killed."

Lynette glared at her. "Then what?"

"I was so scared she'd find me and take me hostage, or worse. That's why I didn't want sirens. If she panicked..."

Susan said, "Good thinking."

Lynette rolled her eyes at her. "You could have called 911and told them no sirens."

"I wasn't thinking straight. I heard what sounded like pictures smashing. I heard glass breaking against the wooden floor. Then she starts ranting."

"Do you remember any of what she said?"

"Some of it was in Spanish, which I don't understand. In English, she said *I was your wife you bastard. You owe me. You got what you deserved.*"

Valerie returned with the water. "Here, drink this."

Madison continued, "I heard the door slam. I heard her running down the steps, but I was so scared. I came out and locked the bedroom door as quietly as I could and I peeked out the window."

Lynette looked up at her. "Did you see anything?"

"Only the car pulling away. An old, blue Volkswagen Beetle." She sipped the water. "I know I should have stayed hidden until you came but like I said, I wasn't thinking clearly."

Susan patted her on the shoulder. "You did great."

Lynette cleared her throat. "Tell me about Harold's ex-wife."

"I had no idea he had an ex-wife. He never mentioned being married before."

Susan said, "Madison told me she and Harold had a whirlwind romance. They didn't know each other for long before they were married, right, Madison?"

"Mom, leave now. You and Valerie both."

Madison said, "No, let them stay. Having them here is comforting."

Lynette sighed and continued taking Madison's statement. "So you didn't know he had an ex. You said you didn't recognize the voice."

"Wait. Maybe …."

Lynette said, "Do you remember something?"

"I was taking out the trash the other day and this woman rolled down her window and asked me questions about the neighborhood. Said she was thinking of buying the house down the street. Oh my God. It was her! That's why the voice sounded a little familiar. She must have been casing the property. I'll bet she's been watching me."

"That's helpful. You can describe her, right?"

"She was short, older, black hair pulled in a bun. I was surprised she was considering that house. I mean, I asked her if she had a family and she said no. The house must have four or five bedrooms. And by the looks of her car and the cheap purse on the seat next to her, it was hard to imagine she could afford the place down the road."

Lynette said, "I see you have security cameras outside. Can you pull up the footage?"

"Cameras. Of course." She got up, then said, "Wait. They only hold the footage for 24 hours. Harold said that's all we needed."

The officer came in. "I dusted for prints. There's glass on the floor by the window and it looks like they were going after the safe. There was a painting on the floor in the office. Looks like it was concealing the safe."

"Was the safe opened?" asked Lynette.

"They didn't open it, but I'll bet they tried. Hopefully we'll come up with some prints."

Lynette said to Madison, "I'll have the patrol car keep an eye out. Lock all the doors, turn on the security cameras. Call me if you remember anything at all. And get someone out here to repair the window, stat. Mom, you can help her find someone, right?"

"Sure. I'll take care of it."

Valerie added, "And we'll help Madison put things back in place."

As Lynette was on the way out, Madison said, "Wait. One more thing."

"Yes?"

"She smelled like she fell into a vat of cheap floral drugstore cologne."

Chapter 24

Valerie dropped off Susan, then went home to start setting up. *Charlie would have loved it here. If he were still alive, he'd have a garden going by now and he'd be out there all the time fussing with it.* She put away some of the kitchen items she'd managed to pack. *This is the kind of house we wanted when Jazmin was growing up but we never could afford it.* The last thing she wanted was to start getting all sentimental about Charlie, the love of her life and partner for 40 years. It hurt too much.

To distract herself, she took the new bath mat and towels into her bathroom, nearly slipping on the wet tile. She put the items on the vanity and bent down to inspect the floor. *Why is there water on the floor? And where's the new towel I put in here yesterday? Who's been in my house?*

She felt jittery and thought about calling Susan, but honestly, she was too tired to keep up with Susan right now and wanted some quiet time to organize the house. *I need a walk to clear my head.* First, she made sure all the windows and doors were securely locked. *Should I call the police, or am I imagining things? Maybe I meant to put the towel in there but didn't.*

Once outside, she calmed herself. *I'll bet the home inspector missed a leaky pipe under the bathroom floor. Great. Like we need more expenses right now.* Her new neighbors rode toward her on adult size tricycles, nearly colliding with her before they were able to stop.

"Valerie? Are you here to stay now?"

"I am. Jazzy and Elijah will be here in a few days."

"Wonderful. You'll have to come for dinner when you all get settled."

"Did either of you see anyone go into my house while I was gone?"

Clara said, "No. Why would someone be in your house?"

"The floor in the bathroom was wet. And I think a towel is missing. Weird. I'm sure it's a leaky pipe."

Tom said, "A leaky pipe isn't likely to leak if no one's been using the water. I can take a look if you like."

"Well, let me see if it happens again."

Tom said, "Come to think of it, I saw a white van in your driveway this morning when I went out to the mailbox. I thought he might have been a plumber or repair man."

"No, I didn't schedule anything. Did the van have a company name on it?"

"No, it was plain white. I saw two guys getting back in and driving off."

"Can you give a description of the men?"

"They looked like ordinary Joes. One was about my height, in shape. The other was tall with bulging arms and calves like trees."

"Anything else?"

"The tall guy was wearing a black baseball cap. Had the Orioles logo on it."

"How could you tell from that distance?" asked Valerie.

"The mailbox isn't so far from your driveway. Besides, I'd know that logo anywhere. I grew up in Maryland and the Orioles are my team."

Clara said, "You should call the police."

Valerie said, "I'm going to do that right now." As soon as Clara and Tom took off on their bikes, she made the call. She debated calling Jazzy, but didn't want to upset her. *She can't do anything from St. Louis, anyhow.*

She paced up and down the sidewalk while she waited for the police. It wasn't long before a patrol car pulled into her driveway.

"I'm the one who called you. Valerie Holmes. I just moved into my new house."

"Officer McGinnis. Tell me what happened. You said there was a break-in?"

"I'm almost sure. The bathroom floor was wet like someone had been in there recently."

"An intruder came in and used your shower?"

"And stole one of my new towels! I know how it sounds."

"No, it's happened before. You do this job long enough you see all sorts of crazy things. What else?"

"My neighbor says he saw a white van parked in my driveway. Two men came out the front door and drove away. One was wearing an Orioles baseball cap."

"When did he see it?"

Valerie said, "Sometime this morning. I wasn't at home all day."

"Did the previous owners clear out all their stuff?"

"Of course."

"One had on an Orioles cap?"

"That's what my neighbor said. Why?"

"It's just…a man in an Orioles cap was captured on security cameras in two recent robberies."

"Not in my neighborhood, I hope."

"Two bank robberies. Orioles fan. You'd think Mets, Yankees—some old diehards still root for the Dodgers in these parts."

"One of the banks was close to here, right?"

"Yeah. And I'll check the footage, but I'm almost sure the security camera across the street from the bank captured a white van. Of course, white vans are a dime a dozen. Was your lock broken? Any sign of a break-in?"

"I don't think so. All the doors and windows were locked."

The officer walked over to the front door. "Were these scratches here before?"

"Honestly, I didn't notice."

Then she followed him around the back. "These sliding glass doors are easy to jimmy. You need a steel dowel to put in the tract."

"Does it look like that's how they got in?"

"Not if it was locked from the inside." He tugged at the door. "I'm guessing they picked the lock on the front door from the scratches I saw."

"My neighbor had seen someone in the back yard last week. And I found a fast food wrapper on the lawn which I'm sure wasn't there when I saw the house with the realtor."

"Hmm. They're looking for something. What fast food place was the wrapper from?"

"The smashed red box looked like McDonald's fries. Why?"

"There's only one McD's on this side of town. I don't know. Together with other info it might help determine the direction they came from, but it's a long shot."

"What were they looking for at a nearly empty house?"

"I don't know."

Valerie said, "The previous owner, Charles Russell, managed the bank that was robbed. Not a coincidence, is it?"

"I'll check it out. Want to call someone to stay with you?"

"I'll be okay. Thanks, Officer. My daughter's going to be working at the Westbrook PD. You'll probably meet her. She's going to partner with Lynette Greene."

"I know Lynette. I was good buddies with her old partner. I'll look out for her. Meanwhile, lock up and stay safe."

Valerie went back into the bathroom and inspected the floor. The grout around the wet area was scratched, just like the front lock. *Looks like someone dug into the grout with a screwdriver.* She wondered if someone had tried to lift the tile.

Clara had seen someone digging in the back yard. *What would you hide under a floor or in a backyard? Money? Bank robbery...bank manager...Chuck Russell. No way the robbers hid the stolen money at the bank manager's house. That doesn't make any sense. Not unless Chuck Russell was in on the robbery and double crossed them. But why would he take off and leave the money behind rather than taking it with him?*

She thought about the second bank. *Was bank manager B in on that robbery?* Her phone rang, startling her. *Calm down. It's just Susan.*

Susan said, "Hey, I hope you weren't in bed yet. I have to tell you something."

"No, just puttering around the kitchen. Someone was in the house earlier." Her voice trembled in spite of her efforts to maintain control. "Might have been related to the bank robbery in the neighborhood. My neighbor saw them in a white van and thought they were delivery people or repairmen."

"Oh my God! Are you okay?"

"They were long gone before I got home. I called the police."

"Do you want to stay with us tonight?"

"No, I'm okay. What did you want to tell me?"

"Madison Chambers called a little while ago. She went into the safe to make sure it hadn't been opened and shut by the intruder. She found letters."

"What letters?"

"From his ex. Threatening letters dating back several months to right before he was killed."

"Did Madison give them to the police?" asked Valerie.

"Yes, and she sent me pictures also. In the letters, Alondra demanded her share of the company and threatened to kill Harold if he didn't cooperate. Even said he should watch over his shoulder because 'you never know what to expect.'"

"What's the woman's name?"

"Alondra Flores Chambers. Return address is in Connecticut. Maybe your friend Jerry can do some digging."

"Shouldn't we leave it to Lynette?" The idea that someone had been in her house made her more cautious than usual.

"Madison is afraid this woman might come after her. She says she told Lynette, but Lynette fluffed it off. Lynette does have a full plate you know. She asked if we could help."

"All right. I'll give Jerry a call and pick you up in the morning. I have some snooping I'd like to do as well. I'd like to have another chat with the manager at the bank across town. Come up with a plan and we'll strategize tomorrow. I'm too exhausted to think now."

Chapter 25

The next morning, Susan called Lynette to tell her Jerry was doing a background check on Alondra Chambers.

"Mom, I've got the letters and we're taking it seriously. Officer McGinnis is handling it. I don't need a private eye's help. We already know where Alondra Chambers lives. We can't arrest someone for sending letters. We haven't even verified it was Alondra who sent the letters."

"But what if Madison's in danger?"

"We're keeping an eye on her house and put an alert out on the ex-wife's car. If she comes into New York through the most direct routes, we will know. I've got to get to work. Stay out of trouble."

Stay out of trouble. Doesn't need the help of a private eye. She pawned the whole thing off on Officer McGinnis. She obviously isn't taking it seriously enough. Susan heard a beep from the driveway, grabbed her purse, and got into Valerie's car.

Valerie said, "The bank manager doesn't get in until 10:00. Why don't we start with Madison?"

"Did Jerry get back to you?"

"I only contacted him last night. He works fast but not that fast."

Susan said, "Imagine finding out your husband had been married before and didn't tell you? I have a hard time believing Madison fell head over heels so fast that her judgement didn't kick in. He was obviously a liar."

"Love is blind."

"That's what they say."

Valerie paused for a moment as if something puzzled her. "And Madison is so pretty. What attracted her to Harold Chambers in the first place? He's not exactly Idris Elba."

"Maybe she saw him as a father figure. Or she was after his money."

Valerie said, "Did you notice some of the photos in her living room? One was a young version of her with a race horse; another was of her and I assume her parents on a yacht drinking champagne. I think she came from money."

When they arrived at Madison's, Susan noticed the puffy eyes and tissue wadded in Madison's hand. "Are you doing okay?"

"About what you'd expect. Thanks for coming so fast. Let me show you the copies I made of the letters. Sit down."

Valerie said, "You hadn't noticed the letters in the safe before this?"

"I never went into the safe. As far as I knew, we had a little petty cash and our passports in there. Harold had also stashed a copy of his will and some other legal stuff inside." She showed them the copies.

Valerie said, "These came in the mail?"

"Yes. I don't know why Harold didn't tell me. Then again, he hadn't mentioned he was married before. He was always trying to protect me."

Susan said, "These are threats, but in order for her to be a suspect, we'd have to show she was in town at the time of the murder."

Valerie added, "And that she was in town when Coach Cullins was murdered. Unless you don't think the two deaths are related."

"Of course, they are. She killed Harold, then found out about Coach being the silent partner. I'll bet she's coming for me next. Then she'll have all our shares."

"Does the will state that?" asked Susan.

"No, but the copy of the will in the safe was made right after we got married. There could have been updates, especially if she were threatening him."

Susan wondered if the updates included his blind daughter, Janalyn. She remembered what Janalyn said about the floral smell at the Succex office. *Cheap, drugstore cologne...*Could Alondra have visited Harold there? And even if she did, would she know he had an addiction to Snacky Sax? Would she have had any opportunity to poison him?

Madison said, "I hope they catch her soon. Once she's behind bars and justice is done, maybe I can start to heal. Imagine an addict with half the company." Madison's phone vibrated. "Give me a minute."

Susan took the opportunity to browse at the photos on the mantle. "You're right. It does look like she came from money. Look at this one with her dad. Isn't that the Sidney Opera House in the background?"

"She's not so young in that one. Looks like it was taken a few years ago. I wonder if her mother is still alive. I'm surprised they aren't here with her."

Madison came back. "Sorry, it was my lawyer. If I find anything else, may I call you?"

"Of course," said Susan. "Hope I'm not overstepping, but are your parents still alive? Maybe they can help you through this."

Madison snapped back. "Not going to happen. They live abroad and, to tell the truth, it's been a while since I've spoken to them."

Outside, Valerie said, "She looked almost angry when you mentioned her parents. I wonder what happened between them."

"Whatever it was, I'll bet if they knew what their daughter was going through they'd be here for her. Do you want to drop by Succex before we hit the bank? I'd like to ask the secretary if Alondra Chambers visited."

"Because of the comment about the perfume?" said Valerie.

"Yeah. I know it's a long shot. You're the driver. If you don't think it's worth it, we don't have to."

"We can make a quick stop. That secretary is going to be mighty surprised when no grandson of mine registers."

When they walked into Succex, they found the secretary behind her desk. By now, she knew them by name.

"Do you need some more information? We're holding an open house next weekend. Maybe you can bring your grandson. I'd love to meet him."

"We'll do that," said Valerie. She pointed to the wilting floral arrangements outside Harold Chambers' office door. "Have the police found Mr. Chambers' murderer yet? I haven't been following the news."

"No. They haven't been back, either."

Susan said, "Most of the time the murder victim knows the killer. Often it's a spouse or significant other who's responsible."

The secretary laughed. "Well, I know Mrs. Chambers would never have killed her husband. They were so good together."

Valerie said, "Did he have children?"

"Just the daughter who founded Snacky Sax. Alissa Chambers. She's married but she kept her maiden name. A lot of women do that these days, especially if they made a name for themselves. He never mentioned an ex-wife, but then again, I never asked."

"Did you notice anyone around here who came to visit him but seemed out of place?"

"No, not that I can remember. And I've got a good memory for faces. Only..."

"What is it?" asked Susan. She felt a flurry of hope in her stomach.

"A few weeks before he died, he asked me to reserve a table at the Italian place down the street. A table for two. He never asked me to do that before."

"Maybe he was meeting his wife."

"No. She dropped by spur of the moment sometimes with food from the deli. That was their lunch thing. Besides, he would have said to make a reservation for him and Madison, not just *reserve a table for two*."

Susan said, "I hope they catch the killer soon."

The secretary turned to Valerie. "I'm looking forward to meeting your grandson next Saturday. Any time between 12 and 5."

Valerie waved on the way out. "That wasn't very helpful."

"Not so fast. A table for two? We know he was fooling around in St. Louis with Sandy at the hotel. I'll bet dollars to donuts he'd done it before. Or it may have been estranged daughter Janalyn. She said she met him at his office. Maybe he took her to lunch."

Valerie checked her watch. "Let's try the bank. Maybe we'll have more luck with the secondary mystery."

Susan said, "The case of the bank robber and the former tenant?"

"Sounds like one of Elijah's *Encyclopedia Brown* titles. What if Chuck Russell hid the money in the house or in the yard and that's what the men in the van are after?"

"If Chuck Russell had a share of the money, I'm sure he wouldn't have left it behind."

"Let's see if this other manager—we'll call him manager B—will talk to us. I don't feel safe bringing Elijah into this."

They pulled into the bank parking lot just as manager B was about to get into his car.

"That's him," said Valerie. "Hurry!" She chirped the car to lock it and hustled.

"What are you going to say to him?"

"Watch." Valerie approached the manager, slightly out of breath from hustling to reach him. "Excuse me, aren't you the manager here? We came by the other day."

"I was just heading out on a minor emergency. If you go inside, one of the girls will take care of you."

"They can't. I need some answers and I'm hoping I'll get them from you."

"What are you talking about?"

"I bought Chuck Russell's house. He was the manager at the bank which was robbed across town."

"I can't say I knew him."

"My new house was broken into. And the neighbor saw someone suspicious in my backyard on another occasion. I'm scared. I think it has something to do with the robbery."

The manager fidgeted. "I've really got to get going."

Valerie pressed on. "I think maybe Chuck Russell was in on the robbery. Maybe he even helped rob your bank, too."

"I doubt it. If he robbed his own, why take a chance at a second location?"

"I don't know, but the men who've been at my place are looking for something and I'm afraid they won't stop until they find it. The silent alarm at the other bank didn't work. Wasn't there a similar issue at yours?"

"Well," he cleared his throat and looked as though he wanted to escape, "Yes, we had a security issue."

"Look, I'm not about to go running to the police with anything you say. I just want to catch the robbers so I can start enjoying my new house. Did the bank robbers approach you and ask you to disable the alarm?"

"I'm highly insulted. Of course not. Now, I have to be going." He pushed past and jumped in his car, then sped away.

Valerie said, "You know he's hiding something. I think he was in on the robbery at this bank just like Chuck Russell was at his bank."

Chapter 26

When Susan arrived home, Mike said, "Jonathan called. They want us to join him and Janet for dinner tonight at Antonio's."

Susan ran through her mind. It wasn't Jonathan's birthday, was it Janet's? No, she had a birthday recently. "What's the occasion?"

"He didn't say. I told him we'd be there. You don't have other plans, do you? Like playing Watson to Valerie's Sherlock?"

"Of course not. But I'm Sherlock, she's Watson." *Technically, she is Holmes. Valerie Holmes. How is it I never noticed the irony?* "Just kidding; of course, I'm available. I wonder if Janet decided to retire?"

Maybe they just want to spend the evening with us over a nice dinner. Any news on the break-in?"

"Not yet. Officer McGinnis is working on it. Really unsettling. We're starting to think Chuck Russell was involved in the bank robbery and double crossed his cronies. That's why he took off so fast."

"In that case, what's in the house? Surely not the money."

"I don't know. That's got us stumped."

"By us, I take it you mean you and Watson?"

"Very funny."

"Go get ready."

"Stay away from the fatty meatballs. They have tons of cholesterol. Did you get in a walk today?"

"Yes. It's been a while since you nagged me about my health. What gives?"

"I want to hold on to you. Valerie misses Charlie; Madison misses Harold. I was so scared when you had your heart attack."

"I'm not going anywhere." He gave her a peck on the cheek. "And while we're at it, don't overdo the carbs. You have to keep your blood sugar down."

She gave a salute. "Aye, aye, sir." After a quick shower, she slipped into a blue cotton sundress with a shawl, and anticipated a relaxing evening.

Antonio's Ristorante. Red and white checkered table cloths, a map of Italy on the wall, and wax-covered Chianti bottle centerpieces screamed classic Italian. Susan smelled oregano and garlic as they followed the hostess into an elegant dining area in the back of the restaurant. Jonathan and Janet sat at a circular table in the corner. Italian opera arias played in the background.

Susan tucked her purse on her lap. "What a nice turn of events. I was planning on making a meatloaf."

Jonathan said, "Glad you could make it on short notice."

"What's the occasion? You've got us dying of curiosity." Susan placed the shawl over the back of her chair. She noticed the sparkle in Jonathan's eyes.

Jonathan put his arm around Janet. "Janet and I are getting married." The sparkle in his eyes spread across his entire face.

Janet said, "He took me out for a picnic and pulled out a ring." She showed her hand.

"Oh, it's beautiful. I'm so happy for you."

Mike shook his hand, then went over to hug Janet. "Congratulations. That's great news."

Susan couldn't help thinking Janet was an upgrade from Audrey, her birth mom. Jonathan hadn't been in her life all that long but she'd felt a closeness to him right from the start which she never quite had with

Audrey. *I'm going to have a step mother!* She contained a laugh. Janet was a decade older than her at most.

Janet said, "We're thinking a small ceremony and a party at our house."

"And sooner rather than later," said Jonathan. "Can't waste time when you get to be my age."

"Nonsense," said Susan. "You have the energy of someone twenty years younger."

Jonathan said, "We invited Lynette and Jason, but Lynette had to work. We'll call them tomorrow."

"I didn't think Lynette was working tonight." *I know she wasn't planning to. That means something major came up, like another robbery or a murder.* She felt a flutter in her stomach like she always did when she pictured Lynette going out to an active crime scene.

"I'm helping her out with a case," said Jonathan.

Susan sat up. "Which case? How are you helping, Jonathan?"

"Lynette's got me looking into the contract for an educational foundation Harold Chambers founded. He listed it as nonprofit but the records aren't adding up."

"When we were giving Valerie a tour of the town, we passed a 5k that was raising money for that foundation."

"Yeah. Its purpose is to give scholarships to the economically disadvantaged, but I can't find paperwork for a single scholarship it funded."

Janet said, "Lynette thinks the money is being funneled through the foundation for tax purposes and diverted elsewhere."

"Otherwise known as money laundering," said Jonathan.

"So who winds up with money now? Madison?" asked Susan.

"She's not listed as an approved account holder at the bank."

"Then who has control of the foundation now that Harold is dead?"

"Lynette's looking into it. More importantly, who knows about the money laundering and can access that money? It's most likely in an off shore account."

Mike said, "Enough shop talk. Pass over the champagne." He poured four glasses. "To the happy couple! May you have many happy years ahead of you." The clinking of the glasses and the glow of candlelight warmed Susan's heart.

On the way home, Susan debated calling Lynette. She wasn't about to mention the engagement. She just needed to know she was safe. And no one ever accused her of not having an overactive sense of curiosity. As she was about to punch in the number, Valerie called.

"Guess what? I heard back from Jerry. I've got info about the ex."

"Well? Don't keep me in suspense."

"Alondra Chambers' most recent address is listed as a halfway house outside of Hartford. She spent time in a drug rehab facility before that. She's unemployed. Jerry got us an address."

"Rehab facility? Drug addict. What's she living on if she's not working?"

"Alimony?" said Valerie.

"Or funds diverted from an educational foundation. I'll explain later. Did he find out if she'd been in New York recently?"

Valerie said, "She made a reservation at the Red Roof Inn in Westbrook. She was in town two weeks before Harold's murder."

"But not closer to the time of the murder?" asked Susan.

"No, but Hartford's only a few hours away. She could have made it out and back the same day. What if she asked him for more money, he said no, and she hatched the poison plan?"

"There are a lot of *ifs* there. Like, was she entitled to a portion of the company since they were divorced, and did she have access to cyanide? And even if she had it, did she have the opportunity to add it to the Snacky Sax?" said Susan.

Mike shook his head at her. "Don't start."

Susan sighed. "I've got to go."

"One more thing. Alondra Chambers purchased a one-way ticket to San Juan, Puerto Rico. Do you want to take a ride to Hartford in my new car tomorrow?"

"I'm game. We'll talk in the morning."

Mike said, "What are you scheming about now?"

"Nothing. Valerie and I are going to take a ride to Hartford tomorrow."

"Not a good idea. First of all, you're meddling. Again. And second of all, what are you going to do if you find the ex-wife? Confront her? You have nothing tying her to the murder. Besides, you have no idea who you're dealing with. I heard you mention rehab. You're going to confront an ex drug addict, accuse her of murder, and think it'll all work out?"

"We aren't going to accuse her."

"That's right, you're not. Because you aren't going."

"We'll be careful. I have to meet this woman and see if she's worth Lynette considering as a suspect."

"It's not your place to do that."

"I'm going. I already told Valerie I would."

"Okay. In that case, I'm coming with you."

Chapter 27

The next morning, Susan *and* Mike waited in the driveway for Valerie. Valerie pulled in and rolled down the window.

"Mike? Are you joining us?"

"Yep. I don't work today so I thought I'd come along for the road trip." He climbed into the back seat. "Did you pick up soda and junk food or do we need to stop at the 7 11?"

"Neither of us needs junk food," said Susan. "Besides, we just had breakfast."

Mike said, "So what's the plan? Show up at the halfway house? They may have restrictions on visitors you know."

"We'll play it by ear," said Susan. She was less than thrilled having Mike chaperone the trip. She tried her best to forget he was in the back and chatted with Valerie. "Hey, last night we found out Jonathan and Janet are engaged."

Valerie said, "Really? That's wonderful."

"Janet's so happy. Her husband died while we both worked at Westbrook Elementary. We stayed close after she transferred to high school and I retired. She had a hard time. When she met my father, it's like the sun came out. She started taking care of herself again. I swear she looks ten years younger now." She looked at Valerie. "I'm sorry. That was insensitive of me."

"No, it's okay. It kind of gives me hope. I can't imagine it now, but maybe someday. Not that anyone will ever be able to fill Charlie's shoes."

"I know." She couldn't help filling the silence. "They have dating sites for people our age."

Mike kicked the back of her seat.

"I'm sorry. I guess I was thinking more for me. That's what I would do if Mike died."

"I've already got my profile on there," said Mike. "Sensitive white male, enjoys working with his hands and long walks on the beach. What was that about poisoning the Sticky Snacks? Cyanide, right?"

"Snacky Sax. Very funny."

Valerie said, "Not to change the subject, but I've been thinking about the bank robbery and Chuck Russell. I can't figure out why he would leave money behind. I don't care what kind of a rush he was in."

Susan said, "And then the second bank robbery. You think the second one happened because something went wrong with the first one?"

"They managed to get the money and avoid arrest, so what went wrong? Maybe we should start searching my house and see what we find."

Mike said, "You know, banks usually safeguard their money from robbery attempts by throwing in a dye pack."

"A what?" asked Valerie.

"A radio controlled dye pack. It explodes after the thief has left the bank and releases dye all over the money so it's unusable."

"They have these sitting in the vaults? Do you suppose Chuck Russell double crossed the robbers by slipping in a dye pack?" asked Susan.

"Why?" asked Valerie.

Susan said, "Either he was being forced to cooperate and did it to trip them up…"

"Or he didn't know it was there," said Mike. "Did he get money from the tellers first or go straight to the vault?"

"I don't know," said Valerie. "But we can find out what they did at the second bank from the other bank manager."

"If they followed the same plan," said Susan.

Mike said, "You might want to mention the possibility to the police. You don't want to tip the manager off and the whole thing is dangerous if the robbers find out you've been nosing around."

"I can't believe they didn't think of that," said Susan.

"Maybe they did, and thought Chuck Russell double crossed them." Mike said.

"Or Chuck Russell didn't expect the dye pack and was afraid of being blamed so he hid the money at the house," said Valerie.

"What money? If we're going on the theory the money became unusable due to the dye, Chuck wouldn't have it. Imagine, they rob the bank holding a gun to Chuck's head, then hand him a sack of money on the way out?" Susan opened her purse and pulled out a bag of M&M's. Valerie held out her hand while Susan poured some into her palm.

Mike said, "If it was covered in dye, the money would be worthless and incriminating at that. The robbers would have wanted to get rid of it right away. And in my opinion, they'd be furious at Chuck for not warning them about the dye pack." He reached over the seat and held out his hand. "Come on, I saw you give some to Valerie. Where's mine?"

Susan poured some into his hand. "Here."

"So, what's your plan when we get to the halfway house? Knock on the door and ask about the ex-wife?" asked Mike.

Susan said, "Don't worry. I've got it covered."

Coming into Hartford, Valerie turned up the volume on her GPS and weaved through lunch time traffic to a quiet street lined with robust trees. "Do you see Coventry Street?"

Susan peered through the window. "Yes, the sign is behind the trees," said Susan.

The wooden two-story was nestled into a suburban neighborhood. From the outside, it looked like any family residential home. No neon sign saying "half-way house."

Mike said, "Well? You're the one with the plan. What's next? Are you sure we can just drop in like this?"

"I researched this place. It's not technically a halfway house; it's a three quarter house for sober living. Residents have freedom as long as they stay drug and alcohol free and they can have visitors. Come on."

Susan knocked on the door, and a young woman wearing jeans and a t-shirt answered the door. "Can I help you?"

"We're here to see Alondra Chambers."

"Alondra? Who did you say you were? Friends?"

"We have some news to pass along to her. News she'll be happy to hear."

"Come in." Valerie and Mike followed Susan into the living room. "Alondra left weeks ago."

"Really? Do you know how we can find her? She's getting a share of an inheritance and we wanted to be sure she claimed it before the nasty relatives tried to cheat her out of it."

"Alondra got a job. She recently finished her biology degree. We were all proud of her going back to school at her age."

"Biology, as in animals and trees?"

"Yes, that's right."

"Is she still in the area?"

"No. She moved out of the country, in fact. Puerto Rico. I suppose technically that's still our country. The rain forest was destroyed by Hurricane Maria in 2017 and they've been hiring people to help rebuild it. She was excited. Good pay and she's originally from San Juan. Win-win."

Susan said, "Was she working here in Hartford before that? You all pay rent, right?"

"Yes, of course. This place isn't some government hand out. We all pay our share. She didn't work because she was going to school to finish her degree, like I said. She was getting support from her ex-husband."

"Like alimony?"

"And more. When she needed tuition money or she had to replace the engine on her car, he helped her out."

"So it wasn't a bitter relationship?"

"No. Believe me, when it's a bitter relationship, you hear about it around here. She seemed to be genuinely fond of her ex. Wish I could say the same about mine."

Mike said, "She got the job and flew directly from here to Puerto Rico?"

"She said she had a stop to make first. I think she was flying out of New York."

"Did you ever meet him? Did he come visit?" asked Susan.

"Not that I remember, and I've been here a long time."

"And you don't have a forwarding address?"

"No, sorry. I hope you find her. I'm sure she'd appreciate the money. It was a relative who died?"

"Yes, in fact it was her ex-husband."

"Oh, she'll be deeply sorry to hear that."

"Let me know if you hear from her. Here's my number." Susan jotted down her number and handed it to the woman. "Oh, and one more thing."

"What?"

"Did Alondra wear a floral scented perfume?"

"Perfume? Alondra? No. She was allergic to almost everything. Scented soaps, lotions, beestings, any type of nuts. All she had to do was smell a peanut and she'd start choking. She had to take an antihistamine if she was going to spend a lot of time around certain plants."

Back in the car, Mike said, "That wasn't what you were expecting, was it?"

Valerie said, "That's not the picture Madison painted at all. Threatening letters?"

"Do you think it's true? Harold was supporting her? They were friendly?" said Susan.

Mike said, "We don't know Alondra. For all we know she made up stories to tell her housemates."

Susan said, "It couldn't have been her outside Harold's office. The blind daughter said she smelled floral perfume when she was in Harold's office."

Valerie said, "What if this woman, Alondra's friend, wanted to paint a good picture. Maybe she was covering for her. Maybe she knew Alondra wanted Chambers dead but didn't want to point the finger at Alondra."

Susan said, "Maybe she helped Alondra kill Harold."

Mike said, "She looked surprised when you said the dead relative was Alondra's husband. I don't think she was lying,"

Valerie said, "Besides, she's allergic to nuts."

Susan said, "Maybe not. Maybe someone else is."

Chapter 28

Valerie rolled over and looked at the clock on her nightstand. 3 A.M. The bank robbery and the fact that someone had been in her house gave her chills in spite of waking up drenched in sweat. *He took a shower in my bathroom! Stole my new towel!* She pulled the pillow over her head. *Not to mention the murder and our trip to Hartford.*

She'd locked her bedroom door. *I never liked the idea of a gun in the house but if Jazzy was here with a weapon, I'd feel safer. Why would the robbers be digging around in my yard or in my bathroom? If Chuck Russell ever had the money he'd have taken it with him, not buried it. Maybe it's time to do a little digging of my own.*

She figured she'd ask Clara where exactly she'd seen someone in the yard and start there, but she'd certainly need help and didn't have any sort of gardening tools. She tossed and turned, eventually drifting back to sleep.

In the morning, she called Susan. "I'd like to start digging in my yard to see what the robbers were looking for."

"How can we do that? I mean, I'm fit enough for my daily…um…occasional…walks, but digging with a shovel? Do you even have a shovel?"

"We can do an inspection. Comb over every inch of that yard and if we find a spot, we'll get help. And what about the other bank manager? Do you think he's got anything buried in his yard?"

"He was hiding something. And he seemed scared. I'll be over in a bit."

Valerie went into the yard and made a plan in her head for how to methodically canvas the yard. Then she walked over to the neighbor's house.

"Hi, Clara, I hope it's not too early to come by."

"Heavens, no. We're both up before the sun most days. Can I help you with something? Come on in."

"Actually, I was wondering if you could come over and take a look in the yard. Do you remember where you saw someone digging?"

"It was right on the other side of our fence." She followed Valerie back to the yard. "Hmm, I think it was right about here. Or here."

Valerie heard Susan's car in the driveway and invited her back. "Clara's showing me where she thinks the digging happened."

Susan bent down. "How about here? This looks a little more disturbed. Clara, is this where you saw him? Do you have a shovel?"

"Looks about right. Tom has a shovel. I'll be right back."

When she was out of earshot, Susan said, "Maybe she should bring Tom as well. How are we going to dig? And it's getting hot already."

As if she read Susan's mind, Clara appeared with both the shovel and her hubby.

Tom said, "I'll get this started. Here?"

At Valerie's direction, he started digging.

Valerie said to Susan, "How about you, me, and Clara transverse the lawn. Each takes a third while Tom digs."

Susan started closest to the house, sweeping her eyes back and forth across the yard but finding nothing unusual. At one point, Valerie thought she'd found something but it turned out to be a sprinkler head.

Tom dug in several places. "I'm not getting anything but dirt." He wiped his brow. "I'll try down a little further but do you really want to ruin all this new sod?"

"One more spot," said Valerie. "I suppose if it's completely undisturbed it hasn't been dug up."

Tom shoveled one more area. "Nothing."

"Okay," said Valerie. "We gave it the old college try. Thanks."

Clara said, "Let me get you home so you can clean up and get a cool drink. Sorry we didn't find whatever it is we were looking for."

"I appreciate your help."

Susan followed Valerie back into the house. "Do you want to go back to the other bank and try bank manager B again?"

"I don't want to seem like we're harassing him."

"Come on, we'll be non-threatening."

When they arrived at the bank, the manager was circulating through the lobby. "You two again? If you aren't here to start an account or otherwise engage in bank business, I'm going to have to ask you to leave."

Susan said, "We don't mean to upset you. My friend here bought a house recently. It was previously owned by the manager at the other bank that was robbed. Someone—we think one of the robbers—has been nosing around in her back yard and even broke into her house."

"He stole my brand new towel," said Valerie.

"What is it you want from me?" asked the manager. "I had nothing to do with the other robbery and my part in this one is over."

"Your part in this one?" said Susan. "We think the robbers were holding something over Chuck Russell's head. They used the information to convince him to help by say, disarming the alarm. We think they did the same to you."

"You have a lot of nerve accusing me of such a thing. I'd never put the safety of my employees at risk like that. Now you need to leave."

Susan said, "Okay, we're going. But if you change your mind and want to do your part in putting a stop to the thieves, you can call my daughter at the police station. Detective Lynette Greene. Do you want her number?"

"Security, come show these ladies out."

"We're going," said Susan. On the way out, she couldn't resist one more try. "Until you find out what's hidden in your house, you're in danger."

Valerie said, "I told you he wouldn't be happy to see us. Did you expect him to admit to being part of the crime? We went too far this time."

"You're right. Come on. I'll take you to lunch. Deli?"

"Deli!"

At the deli, they ordered sandwiches at the counter and carried them to a table.

Susan said, "There's nothing like a garlic pickle. And they make the best potato salad here."

Valerie said, "Should we tell Madison what we learned about Alondra Chambers?"

"Not yet. Let's have another look at those threatening letters. I have photos of them on my phone. Here."

"Let me see that." She pinched it larger and read through line by line. "Didn't the housemate say Alondra was from Puerto Rico?"

"Yeah, why?" asked Susan.

"Look at the dates. Do they look strange?" asked Valerie.

"How? Looks like any other date."

"Exactly. I had a Puerto Rican pen pal when I was in high school and she wrote the date with the day, then the month, then the year. 15/7/20, for example, instead of 7/15/20."

"Maybe after being here in the states she picked up our ways. I wouldn't read too much into it." Susan tucked the pastrami back into her sandwich and took a bite. "And Alondra got her degree in biology. Again, someone with access to making cyanide."

Valerie put down her fork. "So if she knows her way around plants and trees, aren't there easier ways to extract poison than mashing up apple cores to make cyanide?"

"Yes, foxglove and nightshade to name a few," said Susan.

"And hemlock. That's a classic."

"That aside, our theory is that Alondra slipped Harold cyanide because she asked for financial help and he refused. And Madison had no idea that he was married before. Do you buy that?"

"Now that you mention it, it does seem like a stretch. Especially if Harold was sending her alimony checks every month."

"When Madison's house was broken into, the glass from the bay window shattered all over the floor. There was a handle inside the pane. The burglar could have broken the area near the lock, reached in, and unlocked it that way. Why shatter the whole window?

Susan said, "How about you call your friend Jerry and see what he can dig up on Madison Chambers."

"And we can do some of the legwork ourselves. Certainly she's worth a Google search."

"You're right. After lunch we'll get started. Let's grab a couple of black and white cookies to go."

Chapter 29

Valerie put on a pot of coffee and opened her laptop.

Susan munched on a cookie. "We don't know Madison's maiden name. Where do we start?"

"With Harold Chambers. There has to be some sort of wedding announcement, right?" Valerie clicked the keys. "Or a press release when he got married."

"I'll check out her faculty bio." Susan whipped out her phone and went to the SUNY Westbrook website. "Looks like this is her first teaching position; she got her doctoral degree from SUNY Westbrook and it says she's a home grown faculty member."

Valerie said, "I think I've got something. Here's a wedding announcement. Madison Chambers née Madison Bridgeport. Looks like she's a born and raised New Yorker. Her parents are from New Paltz." She searched for more information. "There are a ton of Madison Bridgeports."

"What do we do? Can you call your friend Jerry?"

"Maybe we should go back and talk to Madison again," suggested Valerie. Her phone vibrated. "It's Jazzy."

"Get it. I'm going to get some coffee."

Valerie answered. "Jazzy? Everything okay? Really? Oh, that's wonderful. I can't wait. See you in a few days."

Susan came back into the living room. "Good news?"

"Oh, yes. The moving truck shows up tomorrow and she'll be leaving St. Louis as soon as they take off. She'll be here in a few days. I can't wait."

"Great news." Her phone vibrated. "I guess it's the day for talking to our daughters. It's Lynette."

"Maybe they caught Harold's killer."

"Lynette? Yes, we did talk to the manager. We didn't harass him. He was perfectly willing to talk. Yes, I gave him your number. What? Okay. So I did you a favor. I know. Kiss the girls for me."

Valerie said, "What happened?"

"Our friend, bank manager B, turned himself in. He confessed to Lynette that the robbers threatened to kill his wife if he didn't cooperate." She gave Valerie a high five.

Valerie said, "Does that mean they caught the bank robbers?"

"Not yet."

"What about Chuck Russell? Did they drag him back here?"

"I don't think so. But if news gets out that bank manager B confessed, the robbers may come back here to find what they were searching for. Maybe we should check the front lawn."

Valerie said, "Carmine Vitulli planted the shrubs in front of the house and didn't find any buried treasure. Besides, who buries treasure in the front yard where anyone can see from the street?"

"I'm glad Jazzy will be here soon. I think I'll head home and let you finish unpacking. I want to arrange an engagement party for Jonathan and Janet. I can't decide whether to have it at the house or at a restaurant. Thought I'd call around and check out the possibilities. See you tomorrow?"

"Of course."

"Lock the door behind you." Susan stepped out the front door and missed the stoop. She let out a scream and wound up flat on her back, clutching her ankle.

"Susan, are you okay?" Valerie rushed over. "Don't try to move. I'm calling 911. I'll be right back."

"No, don't call 911. I'm okay." She tried to get up but when she put weight on her ankle it hurt too much."

"Wait there." Valerie brought out a bag of ice wrapped in a new dish towel. "Hold this on it. I called 911. I'll call Mike and tell him to meet us at the hospital."

"Nonsense. I don't need the hospital." She winced. "I feel like an old fool."

"You are not an old fool. Unless, of course, you refuse to go to the hospital. Keep the ice on it."

Susan felt the ankle swelling in spite of the ice. She tried to wiggle her toes, but it sent a wave of pain shooting through her. She thought she heard a siren in the distance.

Valerie ran into the street and flagged down the ambulance. "She's over here."

Two paramedics rushed to Susan's side. One examined the ankle while the other slapped on a blood pressure cuff.

"Ma'am, this appears to be fractured. Let's take you in for x-rays. Easy does it." He supported her weight while the other brought over the stretcher.

"Are you taking her to Westbrook Memorial?" asked Valerie.

"Yes, ma'am."

"I'll follow you. Susan, I'll tell Mike and Lynette to meet us there."

"Don't bother Lynette, she's busy."

"She'll want to know. Now be quiet and do what the paramedics tell you to do."

Susan had to admit it hurt. A lot. She was wheeled into emergency and then to imaging. By that time, Mike and Valerie had arrived.

Valerie said, "I feel awful. You aren't going to sue me, are you?"

"Of course not. I'm the one who wasn't watching where I was going."

Mike said, "Is it broken?"

"They have to see the x-rays."

"Does it hurt?"

"They gave me something for the pain. It's not so bad."

A few minutes later, Lynette rushed in. "Mom, what happened?"

"Twisted my ankle. I wasn't looking where I was going."

The doctor came in. "Mrs. Wiles, there's a fracture. You're going to need surgery to set it."

"Surgery?"

"It's a simple procedure. You'll be out of here in a day or two."

Susan grasped Mike's hand. "How long until I'm up and around?"

"We'll have you up on crutches before you leave, but you'll be in a cast for a good six weeks providing all goes well."

"Goes well?"

"You'll be fine. The nurse will be in with the paperwork and we'll get you admitted."

After the doctor left, Susan digested the fact that she was about to have surgery. The thought of being under anesthesia bothered her as she hated not being in control. She also worried about complications due to her diabetes.

Mike said, "You'll be home in no time. It'll be okay."

"Mom, I'm going to run home and get the girls settled, then I'll be back. Do you need anything?"

"A nightgown, toothbrush, and my Kindle, but Mike can get it."

"I'm not leaving until after your surgery," said Mike.

"I'll run by the house. Did you call Jonathan?"

"I don't want to worry him and Janet."

"He's your father. He'll be mad if we don't let him know." Lynette gave her a kiss on the cheek. "I'll be back."

Susan said, "Valerie, you don't have to stay. Go home and make dinner."

"I guess there's nothing I can do here right now. Mike will let me know when they schedule the surgery, right?"

Mike shook his head. "Of course."

The next few hours were a blur as Susan was prepped for surgery. Her stomach growled but she knew it'd be a while before she could eat and trusted the nurses would keep her blood sugar in check. Her ankle ached as the pain medication began to wear off.

She worried about getting around on crutches, driving, and how she was going to manage the stairs at home.

"I wish I'd get this over with already. I was scheduled to go in an hour ago."

Mike held her hand. "It's not like you're going anywhere on a schedule right now."

"What if I'm not coordinated enough to use the crutches?"

"I'll take some time off to help you manage."

"You've used all your sick days already. I'll be okay. Set me on the couch with the remote and snacks within reach and I'll be fine."

"What happens when you need to get up to go to the bathroom and you drop your crutches? Or you fall and can't get up like on the commercials?"

"Thanks for those pleasant scenarios."

"Maybe Valerie can stay with you for a few hours and I'll work half days."

"I just want to get this over with."

"They'll come get you soon enough."

The anesthesiologist paid them a visit. Susan felt sleepy as transport wheeled her into surgery. Mike was directed to the surgery waiting room, where he called Lynette.

"Lynette, they just wheeled her into surgery now. By the time she's out of recovery, it's going to be late. Just come by in the morning. I'm going to stay here tonight. And do me a favor and call Valerie for me."

Chapter 30

Valerie stood in front of the open refrigerator and, although hungry, nothing looked appealing. She couldn't wait for Jazzy and Elijah to get there. Maybe then she'd feel inspired to cook. Lynette called to tell her not to go back to the hospital until morning.

For the first time since coming to Westbrook, she felt lonely. She missed her friends from her book club and the women in her bible study. And, of course, the ache from missing Charlie was tattooed on her heart forever. *Maybe we should get a dog, like Elijah wants. Of course, Jazzy would have to agree.*

She pulled out a package of Kraft Singles and decided on some good old fashioned comfort food for dinner. Grilled cheese and tomato soup. She was in the middle of warming the soup when she heard a noise outside. Wait. It wasn't outside. It was coming from inside the house! Someone was upstairs. The hair on her neck prickled. It got quiet, then…a bang on the ceiling made her jump. She reached for her phone but realized the last bit of charge was gone. *Fight or flight? A no brainer.* She was about to run outside when she heard the stairs creak. She reevaluated.

I won't be able to make it to the front door without crossing the path of whoever is upstairs. I'll try the back. She tugged on the sliding glass door. Locked, as it should be. She was about to reach down and pull the dowel out of the tract when she heard the footsteps coming closer. *I can hide in the laundry room. Or better, lock myself in my bedroom. I need a weapon.*

She grabbed the iron skillet from the stove, still hot from cooking the grilled cheese sandwich. Then she hid behind the kitchen wall. *It's up to me. Now or never. I'll whack him hard and run out the front door. One, two…*

A man in a black hoodie snuck around the corner and lunged at her, grabbing the skillet while it was still in her grip. She wriggled trying to get loose but it was impossible. His fingers were like handcuffs around her wrists. The hot skillet burned the side of her hand as she fought to get away.

The intruder shouted, "Stop it. I'm not here to hurt you. I didn't hear you come in."

"Let me go. This is assault. With a deadly weapon." She pointed at the skillet with her elbow.

The man let go of her wrists, extricated the skillet from Valerie's grip, and tossed it into the sink. "I'm Chuck Russell. I used to live here."

Valerie caught her breath. "Chuck Russell? Everyone said you left in a big hurry and no one has heard from you. What are you doing in my house?"

"It's a long story."

"I've got time. Unless you want me to call the police right now." Of course, her phone wasn't charged and if he called her bluff she didn't know what she'd do.

"Can we sit and talk this out?"

She sat at the table. "Talk."

"I was the manager of the bank down the road. You may have heard about the robbery that took place there."

"I heard something about it."

"One day when I was leaving the bank, two thugs grabbed me. They said I had to help them rob the bank or they'd hurt my family. They had pictures of my wife and little boy on their phones. I was terrified."

"Why didn't you go to the police?"

"They said if I went to the police, my son wouldn't see his next birthday. I was scared. They promised if I cooperated no one would get hurt."

"And you'd get a share of the money?"

"No. Nothing like that."

"Two men broke in and were digging around your...my backyard. Did they think you buried the money here?"

"No, it's much more involved. One of the tellers slipped a dye pack into the bag with the money before I opened the vault. The money was unusable at that point. They came right into my driveway and threatened me. Said I knew the dye would destroy the money. I swore I didn't."

"Then you went to the police."

"No, not exactly. I quietly put the house on the market and told my wife I'd gotten a better job offer further upstate. We slipped out, but they called me after we left town. Said they were going to implicate me in the robbery if I talked. They said they were going to bury evidence at the house and make it look like I knew it was there."

"What evidence?"

"The soiled money."

"So that's what they were doing. They weren't digging to find something; they were digging to plant it."

"Yeah. I snuck back into town and saw you leave the house earlier. I thought I could find it, but I checked all the places I thought it might be. By places, I mean the attic crawl space and the basement. I didn't see anything."

"We searched the yard. Every inch of it and found nothing."

"They said if I went to the police, besides having my family harmed, I'd be buried up to my neck in this mess."

Valerie got up, opened the blinds on the sliding glass door, and flicked on the light. "Let's check outside and see if we missed anything. What about the roof or the chimney?"

Chuck looked up. "They'd need a ladder. A tall one. Don't you think a neighbor would notice someone up there? And they'd have had to bring their own ladder. I reached into the fireplace and found nothing."

"Buried up to your neck…"

"Wait! The sandbox. Did you dig under there?" said Chuck.

"No."

Chuck ran over to it. "Help me yank this thing up."

First, they dug through the sand. Nothing. Then Valerie grabbed an end and together they jimmied the box over. "I see something!"

Chuck said, "That's got to be it." He pulled out a dirty canvas sack.

"Well, open it!"

Chuck loosened the drawstring and pulled out the stained money. "Mystery solved."

"I can't believe we found it. Now what? You know the manager of the bank across town confessed to helping in the robbery. The police will believe you."

"I plan to go straight over there. I'm tired of being afraid. But…"

"But what?"

"Until the police catch them, my wife and son are still in danger."

"Can you describe the robbers to the police?"

"I think so. But they could be anywhere by now."

"Maybe we need a plan to get them out of commission."

"You've got one?"

"I do. I know someone who can help."

*****

Lynette finished cleaning the dinner dishes and tucked in the girls. "Jason, I'm going to run by my Mom's house and pick up the things she asked for so I can go right to the hospital in the morning."

When she got to Susan's, she poured food into the cat bowls, freshened their water, and went upstairs to the master bedroom where Susan's laptop sat open on the bed. Lynette went to turn it off but when she touched a key, the laptop lit up. A page from a Google search on Madison Chambers stared back at her, making her wonder what her mother was up to.

Something caught her eye. The cursor was on Madison's faculty bio. She clicked on it. She'd never say it aloud, but her Mom's instincts were usually right on. On a pad next to the computer, Susan had written several dates and circled Madison's employment date with an arrow leading to her birthdate.

Lynette knew Madison had been hired right after obtaining her doctorate from SUNY Westbrook. She and Jason had attended a reception for her and the other new hires at the faculty club. Madison looked older than someone who'd gone straight through school. Is that what her mother was concerned with? She'd have been 27 or 28 when she was hired, but that would make her in her early thirties now.

Lynette plugged into the police data base and looked at Madison's driver's license. She was 41 now. What had she been doing in the years between her undergrad degree and her doctorate?

Her phone vibrated in her pocket. "Valerie? Everything okay?"

"I'm sitting here with Chuck Russell, the former bank manager and previous owner of my home."

"I know who he is, but what's he doing there?"

"It's an interesting story. He's not guilty. He was forced to participate in the robbery and was scared so he skipped town. He was being threatened."

"Valerie, you could be in danger."

"He wants to help."

"Have him meet me at the station."

"Actually, I have a better idea."

Chapter 31

Valerie paced back and forth until she heard Lynette pull into the driveway. She turned to Chuck and said, "I think this is your lucky day. The threat of the robbers will be behind you, and the bad guys will be locked up in jail."

"Glad I didn't erase the phone message so I have a way to contact them."

Valerie let Lynette in. "Let's get started."

Lynette said, "You have no idea how far away these guys might be. I'm not sure this will work, but I've got Officer McGinnis on standby just in case. Chuck, do you know what you're going to say?"

"I do. Should I call now?"

"Go for it. Put it on speaker."

Chuck punched in the number and the call was picked up on the second ring.

A gruff voice said, "What do you want? Remember, if you say anything I'll point the cops straight at you and there's evidence linking you directly to the crime."

"That's what I wanted to talk to you about. I have a confession to make. I pocketed some of the cash from the vault before I started shoveling it into the bags. I've got a stack of thousands. Useable thousands."

"You lied to us?"

"Yeah, but I'm going to make you a deal. I don't want to live looking over my shoulder. If you meet me at my house, I'll trade you the clean money for the evidence you planted and we'll go our separate ways."

There was silence. Then the gruff voice said, "You better be telling the truth."

"I swear on my son's life."

"Your son's life is already in danger. We'll be there in an hour. Be alone or he dies."

"I am."

When he hung up, Lynette immediately contacted Officer McGinnis. "It's a go. Come on over. Bring back-up. And bring a few stacks of thousands with you from the station. In a big manila envelope. Hurry." She turned to Valerie. "I need you to leave." She reached into her pocket. "Here's the key to my mom's house. I don't want you here; it isn't safe."

"I don't want to stay alone. I'll lock myself in the bedroom and I won't make a peep."

"If he finds out someone else is here, you'll put all our lives in danger."

"I swear; I'll lock the bedroom door and hide in the bathroom. I'll lock that door, too. When it's all over, bang on the bedroom door."

Lynette shook her head. Then she went over the plan with Chuck. "Don't let on that you know it was hidden under the sandbox. Act surprised. I'll be right here in the laundry room. Officer McGinnis and his partner will be hiding outside. You have to get him to look under the sandbox and we can arrest him."

Officer McGinnis and his partner practically performed a miracle getting the cash together so quickly. Lynette warned Chuck. "You don't let him have it before he goes into the yard."

"Won't he want to see it? It doesn't look like much."

"He has to believe you snuck it out of the vault without them noticing. Give him a glimpse but don't let him run out with it before he incriminates himself."

Valerie trembled, partially from fear; partially from the excitement. "I hear a car."

"Get in the bedroom and lock the door. Not a peep. It's show time." Lynette hid in the laundry room and was able to see into the kitchen through the slats in the door. Officer McGinnis and his partner hid in the back yard. Valerie's heart quaked when she heard the knock on the front door.

Chuck answered. "Come in. Let's get this done. Give me the evidence, I'll hand you the money."

"First you show me the cash."

Chuck led him into the kitchen and grabbed the envelope from the counter. "It's all there. Everything I could grab without you noticing."

The robber seemed satisfied. "Let's go. In the yard."

Chuck opened the sliding glass door. "Well? Where is it?"

The robber made a bee line for the sandbox. "You better not try to pull anything. If that money has a tracker in it, I'll tell the cops you were the mastermind behind the whole thing." He reached under the sandbox.

Officer McGinnis stepped out of the shadows. "Hold it right there."

The robber ran away, and right into Lynette's path. "You're under arrest. The officers will read you your rights. If you cooperate and help us catch your partner in crime, the system may go easier on you."

Officer McGinnis and his partner cuffed him and took him to the patrol car.

Chuck said, "Thank you. I have my life back."

"Not so fast. Charges can still be made against you for your involvement, but your cooperation will go a long way." She banged on Valerie's door. "You can come out now."

Valerie said, "All done? You caught them?"

"Caught *him*. There's another one out there but if this one squeals on his pal—which I have a feeling he will—it's case closed."

"I'll have a lot to tell Susan at the hospital tomorrow."

"She'll be sorry she missed it," said Lynette.

"What about bank manager B?"

"Huh?"

"The one who confessed."

"He and Chuck have similar stories. Tonight corroborates the circumstances. I think they'll get off lightly."

"We made a good team, right?"

"Don't get any ideas." Lynette smiled. "But Jazzy would be proud of you."

Chapter 32

It took Susan a moment to realize where she was when she woke up with her ankle throbbing. A nurse stood over her, pumping a blood pressure cuff.

"How are you feeling this morning? How's your pain level?"

"I'd say a five. My throat hurts."

"It's from the anesthesia. Here. Sip some water."

"How long will I be in here?"

"The doctor will come by this morning. It depends on how you're doing and if we can get you up on crutches. Your daughter's outside. I'll send her in." She wheeled the machine away from the bed and out the door, passing Lynette.

Lynette set an overnight bag by the bed. "I brought the things you wanted. How do you feel, Mom?"

"Not too bad. Did I miss anything?"

"You missed a lot. Last night, we caught one of the bank robbers. And we've got a confession from Chuck Russell."

"Really? How did you manage that?"

"Chuck Russell snuck into Valerie's house. The robbers threatened him by planting evidence of the robbery at the house. Valerie confronted Chuck Russell, called me, and we set a trap to catch the robbers."

"The robbers planted evidence? Valerie was there?"

"Yes. I made her lock herself in her bedroom while we carried out the plan. She's every bit as stubborn as you are and refused to go wait at your house. I'll let her fill you in on the details."

Susan felt strangely disappointed at missing out on the excitement. "Now she doesn't have to worry about anyone sneaking around her house. Next we have to tackle the murder case. Any progress?"

Lynette, in a moment of weakness after seeing her mom immobile in the hospital bed sporting a cast, played along. "When I went by to get your things, I noticed you were researching Madison Chambers. Any particular reason?"

"Valerie and I spoke to someone who lived with Alondra Chambers, Harold's first wife. Their stories don't match. Madison says Alondra was threatening Harold. She even showed us letters that had been sent over. And there was the break-in. Madison thought Alondra was responsible." She was glad Lynette didn't ask for details and grill her about going to Hartford.

"What did the friend say?"

"She had nothing but good things to say about Alondra. And yes, she bought a ticket to Puerto Rico, but it wasn't to flee the country, it was to start a new job."

"We had already checked into Alondra Chambers and had no reason to put her on the suspect list. What's interesting is Madison's take on her."

"What do you mean?"

"Madison never reported any threatening letters, nor did she mention thinking Alondra broke into her house. Did Madison ever mention where she was between getting her undergraduate degree and starting the job at SUNY Westbrook?"

"I assumed she went straight through and was hired right away. What did Jason say?"

"He knows she did her doctorate and moved into the office next to him when she got the job. He doesn't know anything before that. You know how Jason is. Not much for chit chat. Checking her age against what we know, she didn't go straight through school. And she has no history of prior employment."

"Valerie noticed something odd. The letters Madison showed us from Alondra had the dates written like we do, but Alondra grew up in Puerto Rico. They put the day before the month."

"In and of itself, it could be nothing. Maybe she picked up the habit when she moved here."

"And Valerie saw glass outside the window. Wouldn't it have shattered inward?"

"If the impact was hard, pieces could have sprung back into the yard. I found it strange also, but when I checked in with an expert at the station, I found out it's not that unusual." Lynette folded her arms across her chest.

"The problem is motive. Madison was living the good life with Harold—tennis lessons, a beautiful home. And she seemed genuinely distraught when he died."

"She certainly had the opportunity to poison him, but I'm at a loss for a motive. *I* will investigate further." She looked at Susan emphasizing the word *I*. "I almost forgot." She dug in her purse. "Annalise made you a get-well card."

Susan opened the folded paper with the big heart on the cover. "What a sweetie. This is me and her baking together. Tell her thanks."

"Look closely. See the flames around the oven door? I'd better get to the station. I'll drop by after work."

Susan closed her eyes and imagined the scene at Valerie's house. *The robbers weren't looking for something, they were planting it. Interesting.*

When she opened her eyes, Mike was standing by her bed holding a white paper bag. "I brought you a bagel. I remember how awful hospital food can be."

She gave him a kiss. "Thanks. Lynette just left. Sounds like I missed some excitement."

"I'd say breaking your ankle and going through surgery is excitement enough. You feeling okay?"

"Yeah. Not too bad. I should be able to come home tomorrow."

"You think you'll be able to get around on crutches or should I ask for a wheelchair?'

"I won't be caught dead looking like a pathetic old lady who needs a wheelchair because she can't figure out crutches. And by the way, just because I'll be out of commission for a while isn't an excuse for you to stop taking walks around the neighborhood."

"With you home 24/7, believe me, I'll take those walks."

"I'd hit you if I could reach." She took the bagel out of the bag. "Now this is breakfast."

After Mike left, the rest of the morning was a whirlwind of visits from her doctor, nurses, and a physical therapist. Every time she shut her eyes, someone new was in the room. She longed to go home so she could rest. Valerie stopped by and told her all about last night and how she heard on the news that the second robber had been picked up. After she left, Susan turned on the TV and dozed on and off.

Close to dinner time, a patient around her own age was wheeled in and put in the second bed. Her arm was in a cast and she was anxious to talk.

"Hello, roomie. I'm Cheryl. I'd shake hands, but…." She picked up her arm and laughed a gruff laugh.

"Susan Wiles. I had ankle surgery last night."

"It's going to be tough. Is that your right ankle? At least I broke my left arm and will still be able to manage most things."

"If you consider breaking a bone lucky at all."

Cheryl turned her attention to Susan's TV. The news was on. "Turn it up. Look, they had a funeral today for the Succex guy who was murdered. That's his wife, the grieving widow in black. Hah."

Susan was puzzled by her reaction. "Hah? The poor man is dead and the widow is grieving."

"You mean the black widow."

"What are you talking about?"

"Don't you remember? Maybe you wouldn't. It's been a few years since it happened."

Susan wanted to reach into her mouth with forceps and pull out the words." A few years since what happened?"

"Since she got off the hook for murdering her first husband. She poisoned him, just like she did this one. They couldn't prove it so she walked. Just like OJ Simpson."

"I sort of remember. It didn't happen around here, did it?"

"No, it was in New Jersey when little missy there was a student at Rutgers. She got involved with a much older business tycoon. Julian Fountainbleu. They were married maybe a few months when he keeled over dead. I'm a bit of a true crime buff. Some would call me a fanatic."

"If she poisoned him, how did she manage to avoid jail?"

"They couldn't prove it. He died while he was away on a business trip. First they thought it was a heart attack, but the man's son, Regence Fountainbleu, insisted on an autopsy because he suspected the wife. Turns out there was poison in his system."

"You think she poisoned something he took with him when he traveled?"

"A special cigar he brought with him. Sound familiar?"

"And no one around here put this together?" asked Susan.

"She changed her last name and it didn't happen in Westbrook."

Impressive, if she's credible. "How do you know all this? Are you a private eye or a detective?"

Cheryl laughed with her smoker's voice. "Like I said, I'm a true crime buff. It's all there if you know where to look."

"So Madison inherited her first husband's estate?"

"Yep, half of it. His son got the other half and vowed he'd prove it was murder and claim the rest."

"Interesting."

"Want to know my secondary theory?" She didn't give Susan a chance to answer. "I think the son tried to set Madison up for her latest husband's murder."

"Why not just kill Madison?"

"Too obvious. If he heard she'd remarried and was heir to a second fortune, it would have ticked him off. And you know what they say. Revenge is best served cold."

A nurse came in to attend to Cheryl and pulled the curtain around the bed. Susan's immediate impulse was to call Madison. Madison picked up on the first ring.

"Madison, just calling to check in on you. I know the funeral was earlier today. I'd have come, but I'm in the hospital with a broken ankle."

"Oh, no. Sorry to hear that."

"I'll be going home tomorrow. Look, I was working on the suspect list. Anyone else besides Carmine and Bruno Vitulli you can think of who may have killed your husband? Think hard."

"I don't know. Maybe another angry parent? Or an investor?"

"Do you think it's possible someone murdered Harold to frame you for the murder?"

"Like who?"

"You were married before. Your first husband was poisoned. You were a suspect."

"I try to keep that confidential. I was a suspect thanks to his ungrateful son, Regence."

"What do you mean?"

"His son insisted I poisoned his father. The police investigated. I was totally cleared."

"So he carried a grudge, seeing you get off the hook?"

"Yes, but after all this time? I don't know. He *was* seething mad."

"Succex has been in the news lately. Maybe it rekindled the grudge and he saw a way of nailing you for Harold's murder."

"You think he framed me? Do you think I'm in danger?"

"You should contact Detective Greene and tell her."

"I'll do that. Hope you feel better, soon."

Chapter 33

In the morning, the physical therapist worked with Susan, who felt shaky, more from fear of falling than from having had surgery. The older she got, the more vulnerable she felt and she didn't like it at all. Her sleuthing hobby helped keep her mind sharp, even if her body was starting to show its wear and tear. By early afternoon, she was ready to be discharged.

Mike pointed to the crutches. "You sure you can use those things?"

"Yes, the physical therapist says I'm a pro. Made it all the way down the hall and back."

A nurse came in with instructions and a wheel chair. "You're ready to go. Keep it elevated and you've got a prescription for pain meds. Call us if you have any problems. Your husband can bring the car around."

Cheryl said, "Taking off so soon?"

"I don't know if taking off is the right word, but I'm going home."

"Remember, when you hear hooves, think horses not zebras."

Susan scooched into the wheel chair. In the elevator, Mike said, "What was she talking about? Zebras and hooves?"

"The most obvious choice is usually the correct one."

Mike drove home, got her settled in the living room, and said, "I need to run by work for a couple of hours or so. You going to be okay? Maybe Valerie can come by."

"I'll be fine."

"Didn't look like you were handling those crutches so well coming in from the car."

"Well, enough to get from the couch to the bathroom and the fridge. Give me the remote and I'm set."

He handed her the remote, brought in her water bottle and pain meds, then tucked an afghan around her. "Here's your phone. I'll be back soon." He kissed her goodbye.

She turned on the TV and must have dozed off. She woke to the sound of the doorbell.

"Coming." *Slowly.* She squinted through the peephole. "Madison? Come on in."

"These are for you." She held a pan of brownies. Susan struggled to balance herself in such a way that she could carry them. Madison walked toward the coffee table. "I'll set them down for you."

"What brings you here?"

"Our conversation last night. Did you tell anyone your theory about Julian's, my first husband's, son being Harold's killer?"

"Not yet. Have a seat." Susan hobbled back to the couch.

Madison said, "I try to keep it under wraps, especially now. I can just hear the buzz about the black widow who killed two husbands. But the more I thought about it, the more plausible it seems."

"Did they arrest anyone for your first husband's murder?"

"No, the case is still open. I think his son, Regence, did it. I was the perfect scapegoat."

"Regence killed your first husband, his father, and then killed your second husband, Harold, to frame you for murder?"

"Yes. Regence and his dad had a horrible falling out just before Julian was killed."

"Over what?"

"Regence had just been charged with a DUI. Julian felt he was too irresponsible to handle the business, rewrote his will, and cut him out. However, if I die or am unable to run the company, for example, if I go to jail, Julian inherits the company."

"You're running a company along with teaching at the university?"

"I hired a business manager and, in actuality, have little to do with it."

"Did you tell the police your theory?"

"Of course, I told them, but they didn't take it seriously. Regence must have found out I remarried and he's out for revenge."

"How did Regence get access to cyanide and plant it in the Snacky Sax?"

"Everything's available online these days. He could have tampered with the Snacky Sax at Succex. With the parents and prospective students in and out, he could have gone unnoticed. Or maybe he was at the conference in St. Louis."

Feasible. Look how easy it was for Valerie and me to make up the story about Elijah. "What about Mark Cullins? Why kill him?"

"Do we know for sure the two murders are related? What if Cullins was stabbed in the locker room for his fancy watch or the keys to his Tesla and the killer was interrupted before he could take the item?"

"I never considered that."

"Anyway, I wanted to let you know I'm selling the house and moving across the country to Alaska."

"Alaska?"

"I have an aunt and uncle there. They're getting older and offered to let me stay with them. It's a win-win. I can help them out."

"Moving across the country is certainly a fresh start. I know a real estate agent if you need one."

"Thanks. I'm having a huge garage sale this weekend. Why don't you and your friend come by."

"I'm sure Valerie will find things she can use for the new house. We'll be there."

She took out a piece of scrap paper from her purse. "Here's Regence's contact information, in case you and your friend want to do some nosing around."

As soon as Madison left, Susan was on the phone with Valerie. "Can you come over? I think I've got a new lead. Madison's first husband's son has motive and made a threat."

"I'm not sure I followed what you just said, but I'll be right there."

Meanwhile, Susan sketched out a suspect chart *Carmine Vitulli, Alondra Chambers, Madison Chambers, and now Regence Fountainbleu. Regence Fontainebleau. Carmine had a strong motive and access, but he seems like such a nice guy. Alondra, according to Madison, made threats because Harold was giving her money but Madison refused to. She fled to Puerto Rico. Or went there for a job, depending on who you believed.*

Madison had means but what motive? She was in this same position once before, however, when her first husband was poisoned. Was she a black widow gathering fortunes? And now she's moving across the country.

That leaves, Regence Fountainbleu. He threatened revenge back when his father was killed and Madison was cleared. He has a DUI on his record and was angry at his father for leaving the business to Madison. He'd inherit it, however, if Madison were to die or be put in prison.

She heard a knock and let Valerie in.

"I brought you cookies. How are you feeling?"

"Not too bad."

Valerie followed her to the couch and looked at the chart. "Someone's been busy!"

Susan went through her chart with Valerie. "We need to focus on the newest suspect. Regence Fountainbleu."

"When you called last night, I did a search. Regence doesn't have a job, and looking at his social media, he's running through his father's money drinking and partying. Pictures of him in bars and clubs all over his posts. And he posted about breaking up with a girlfriend, getting thrown out of her apartment and becoming a *sofa surfer*. I didn't know that was a thing."

"So he no doubt needed money. Is he still living in New Jersey?"

"I checked out some of the clubs and bars he recently posted about. They're all in New Jersey."

"So he'd have had to come to New York about three weeks ago. With cyanide and access to Snacky Sax. Can you…"

"Call Jerry? Already did. He's working on it."

The phone rang. "Janet? Yes, I'm feeling okay. Glad to be back home. I was going to do the party for you! Okay. We'll be there."

Valerie said, "What was that about?"

"I feel bad. I was going to plan an engagement party but sounds like she already did."

"That'll be fun. It's encouraging to see them happy. Maybe someday I'll feel up to meeting someone, but right now it's hard to imagine."

"I haven't met Jerry, but he's always right there when you ask for help."

"He and my hubby were best friends, so I think he feels a sense of duty or something."

"Is he married?"

"What? No. He lost his wife years ago."

"I'm just saying…"

"I don't want to talk about it."

Chapter 34

The next day, Valerie picked up Susan to go to Madison's yard sale.

"Feeling better rested?" said Valerie.

"Yes, I slept most of yesterday. Had to make up for all the sleep I lost while in the hospital. You must be excited about Jazzy and Elijah arriving tomorrow."

"You bet I am. I'm hoping Madison's selling off her lawn mower. I know we're going to need one."

"Hate to break it to you, but I'm fairly certain she'd have used a lawn service."

When they got to Madison's, the front lawn was full of early birds. Susan said, "Pull up on the grass like the others seem to be doing." A couple fiddled with fitting a space heater into the backseat of their Camry.

Well organized tables held books, kitchen appliances, and knickknacks. Racks of clothing and baskets of blankets and decorative pillows filled the grass like lawn chairs at an outdoor concert. In the garage, there were power tools, skis, and the lawn mower Valerie had hoped to find. While Valerie haggled down the price, Susan leafed through the racks of clothing. *A fur coat? She might need that in Alaska. And this Norwegian cable knit sweater?* A shopper searching next to her grabbed a cashmere sweater and a snake skin belt.

Valerie tapped her on the shoulder. "I got the lawnmower and a snow blower for practically nothing. We have to wait until the crowd clears out to get it out of the garage."

"There are some kitchen items on that table. Need anything?" Susan hobbled over to the next table.

"Look at this old silverware collection. I'll bet it's worth something."

"The pattern is beautiful but getting the tarnish off would be a chore."

Valerie said, "Here's a set of butcher knives. I'm hoping to convert Jazzy to a mostly plant based diet like you and I are trying to follow so I don't need those." She picked one up. "Looks expensive."

"One of them is missing so it's not quite a set. It would bother me having three knives and four slots sitting on my kitchen counter." Susan hobbled to the next table.

"You look like you're in pain," said Valerie. "We can go. I'll come back later for the mower and snow blower."

"No." She looked around. "There's a folding chair over on the side of the garage. I just need to sit for five minutes." She hobbled toward it, Valerie closely behind.

"You don't have to hover. I'm not going to fall." She worked her way into the chair. "Go, explore. I'll be fine. All the good stuff is going to be gone if you don't hurry."

"It's pretty well picked over already. I'll be back in five minutes."

Susan felt her ankle itching and wanted to scratch right through the cast. Then she heard a voice coming through the open window above her. Sheer curtains floated in the breeze. She recognized Madison's voice.

Madison said, "That's right. Liquidate it all. I'll send you the account information. Right away."

She's on the phone with someone. Liquidate what?

"When it's done, close out the foundation and delete all the files. Yes, I said all."

I'll bet she means the educational foundation Harold founded.

"As for the company, transfer all the assets and file the bankruptcy paperwork. Got it? Good. Let me know when it's complete."

Susan's pulse exploded with adrenaline.

Valerie came over. "Feeling better?"

"Yes. And you'll never believe the conversation I just heard."

"Tell me."

Susan leaned in. "Madison was talking to someone on the phone. She's liquidating her assets, having the funds transferred to some secret account, and declaring bankruptcy for Succex."

"You're kidding? So she's the silent partner."

"And she's about to flee. Not to Alaska. If you were going to move to Alaska, would you sell your snow blower and expensive sweaters? What about a fur coat? I think she's heading for the Cayman Islands."

"Why the Caymans?"

"I just threw that out because of the secret account. Isn't that where they have off shore accounts?"

"Or Switzerland. You don't hear so much about Swiss bank accounts these days." Valerie helped her out of the chair.

"But you'd need a fur coat in Switzerland."

Valerie's phone vibrated. When she saw Susan was steady on the crutches, she answered. "Hey, Jerry. Really? Yeah, I appreciate it. Yeah, I'm getting settled and Jazzy and Elijah are arriving tomorrow. I'd like that. Thank you."

Susan noticed Valerie's smile. "What was that about?"

"Regence Fountainbleu spent the last month crashing with a friend at a beach house in Maine. And social media confirms he wasn't in Westbrook when Mark Cullins was stabbed, either."

Susan said, "So he's off the suspect list. You said stabbed. I'd forgotten Mark Cullins was stabbed. Remember the missing butcher knife from the set? I'll bet that isn't a coincidence. Everything else Madison had was intact and organized. How'd she lose a butcher knife?"

Valerie said, "Let's get home. I'll come back for the mower later. Or not. The crowd has really thinned out and the tables are practically empty."

As they headed to the car, Madison stopped them. "I'm closing up shop now. You can get the mower and snow blower now so you don't have to make another trip. Come on, Valerie if you could grab the sign, I'll bring the few remaining items into the garage."

The lawn cleared quickly. Susan's instinct was to hobble to the car and forget the mower, but Valerie followed Madison into the garage and Susan didn't want to abandon her.

Madison said, "Valerie, go get it started. I'll clear a path. Susan, there's a folding chair if your ankle's bothering you." Madison disappeared behind a stack of cardboard cartons.

Susan sat, her ankle aching. "Psst. Valerie. Let's get out of here. I have a bad feeling."

"It'll just take a few minutes. Do you know how expensive new lawn mowers and snow blowers are?"

"What's that noise?" said Susan.

The garage door closed. Madison came out from behind the cartons holding a remote in one hand, a gun in the other.

"Madison, what are you doing?" shouted Susan.

"Valerie, go stand by Susan. Susan, for a snoop, you are awfully careless. If you heard me through an open window, didn't you realize I could hear you telling Valerie about my phone conversation?"

"What conversation?"

Madison said, "Don't play stupid. You know I killed Harold so I could have full control of the company, right? And that the foundation was established to funnel money out of Succex."

"If you and Harold were partners, why did you have to kill him?" asked Valerie. She reached in her pocket and while Madison explained, hit redial hoping by some miracle Jerry would pick up and catch on to what was happening.

"Mark Cullins was right. Harold should have laid low with the bribery. The authorities were closing in. He was about to be arrested for his actions."

"Then why kill Mark Cullins if he was trying to convince Harold to lay low?" asked Susan.

"He was going to go to the police and confess his part in the scheme. You don't think he bought a Tesla on a coach's salary do you?"

Valerie said, "So you stabbed him with the butcher knife before he could confess at the press conference."

"You got it. If you'd only kept your noses out of this I wouldn't have to kill you."

Valerie said, "You don't. Go off to the Cayman Islands and we won't talk. We'll stay locked up in your garage while you flee the country, Madison." *Please, Jerry. I'm praying you hear this.*

"Right. Both of your daughters are detectives to boot."

Susan said, "How about you try Valerie's plan? Lock us in and when you're safely out of the country, call Lynette to rescue us."

"Good try." She aimed the gun at them with one hand and grabbed a red gas can with the other. "Sorry, ladies but this is how it has to be." She sprinkled gas across the garage.

Susan's eyes darted from the gas can to the gun. *If Madison owns a loaded gun, why did she stab and not shoot Mark Cullins?* She squinted through her bifocals. *Maybe it's not loaded.* She caught Valerie's eye, wishing she could make her understand what she was thinking. She bobbed her head in the direction of the crutches as if employing Morse Code. Valerie mouthed 'crutches' and Susan nodded.

In her bravest voice, Susan said, "I think if you wanted to kill us you'd have shot us by now."

Madison stopped sprinkling the gas. She stepped toward them, gas can in hand. Susan held her breath for as long as she could to avoid smelling the fumes.

"You really want to try me? Inhaling smoke must be less painful than being shot."

While she spoke, Valerie grabbed one of the crutches like a baseball bat and lunged at Madison, hitting her hard on the head. Madison slipped on the slick floor. The gun flew from her hands and landed in a puddle of gasoline. Valerie, pulse beating like a metronome on steroids, scrambled to the side door, turned it, pulled it...locked. Her heart sank. She eyed the garden tools hanging from the garage wall.

Madison stumbled to her feet. Valerie grabbed a shovel and swung. Madison ducked, avoiding the blow. Madison wrestled the shovel from Valerie, threw it on the cement floor and grabbed Valerie's wrists. The garage remote fell out of Madison's pocket, landing with a thud.

"You think an old lady like you is a physical match for me? You're just prolonging the agony." She pulled Valerie deeper into the garage by her wrists. Susan grabbed the other crutch and wacked Madison over the head. Valerie pulled free and grabbed the garage remote, which was closer than the gun. Praying the hard crash against the cement hadn't broken it, she pushed the button to open the garage door. *Thank God!* She and Valerie ran toward the light beginning to illuminate the garage.

"Susan, it's opening. Run for it."

Susan did her best to balance and worked her way to the door. She heard Valerie breathing behind her. She was almost out when she heard Valerie scream.

Madison had gotten a hold of Valerie's ankles and was dragging her further into the garage. "Man, you're heavy." The garage door was now open halfway.

Madison let go of one ankle for a moment to recover the remote. Valerie kicked but couldn't break free. A millisecond later, Madison held both ankles firmly once again and pressed the remote.

The garage door began to close, blocking the sunlight. Susan dropped to the ground and rolled under it just in the nick of time. Pain seared through her shoulder. She heard the door crash down. Valerie was still inside. The door crept upward an inch. Susan panicked, wondering if Madison would come out after her.

She hobbled as fast as possible toward the neighbor's house. The smell of smoke crept up her nostrils. Over her shoulder, a dirty cloud formed a growing veil across the garage.

Coughing with every step, she continued toward the neighbor's house. She heard the garage door. Stumbling across the lawn, she tried to scream but only managed to choke on her own breath.

Then she heard sirens.

Chapter 35

A week had gone by and everything looked brighter. The sun shone in a cloudless sky and Susan felt a breeze whisper through her hair as she and Mike walked up to Jonathan's home.

Janet opened the door. "Come on in. Jason, Lynette and the girls are in the living room." Janet wore a satin, ivory dress with cap sleeves and a bit of lace on the bodice.

"You look beautiful." Susan said, "I love the way you did your eyes with the sparkly shadow. What's the occasion?"

"Grandma!" Annalise ran up to her. "Can I try your crutches again?"

Lynette shot her a look.

Susan answered, "No, honey. You might get hurt."

Jonathan said, "Have a seat. The minister will be here shortly."

Lynette said, "Minister? I thought you invited us here for lunch?"

"Surprise," said Janet. She clutched Jonathan's hand. "We're getting married."

"Today?" said Susan.

"We didn't want to wait another day. Annalise, do you think you can hold these flowers and be my flower girl?" She handed her a bouquet of daisies.

"Yeah! I've been practicing for Uncle Evan's wedding."

"Oh, you're gonna be an old pro by then," said Janet.

"Hopefully she'll still be young enough to be a flower girl by the time Evan and Cara get their plans together." Susan tousled her granddaughter's hair.

While they waited for the minister, Janet said, "It's always good to have someone looking out for you. Imagine if Jerry hadn't responded when he heard what was going on through Valerie's phone. Imagine if Lynette hadn't gotten to Madison's in time to get Valerie out of the garage before the fire got out of control."

"It was more than a little scary trying to hobble over to the neighbor's house with this cast on. I'm glad Valerie thought so quickly to redial Jerry."

Jason said, "Madison, huh. I guess you never know."

"I should have realized something was off earlier when Madison made a comment about an addict getting half the business. She swore she didn't know Harold had been married before. There's no way she would have known Alondra was an addict."

Jason said, "I guess the university will be doing a faculty search. By the way, what happens to Succex? Are they still going bankrupt?"

Jonathan said, "I received a call from Janalyn, the illegitimate daughter if that's still the term. Harold Chambers amended his will after realizing he had a daughter. He stipulated that the company go to her in the event Madison was unable to run it. She's a biology major, but has a minor in business."

Susan said, "That's great. I'm glad she kept the card I gave her."

"And Harold left a generous lump payment to Alondra, his ex."

Janet said, "In other news, Bruno Vitulli stopped by the library the other day. Harvard admissions heard about the scandal and offered him a place in the upcoming freshman class. Isn't that great?"

"With a scholarship, I hope," said Susan.

"Here's the best part. Harvard doesn't want its students graduating with massive student loan debt. Families that make under a certain income attend tuition free."

"How are Jazmin and Elijah settling in?" asked Janet.

Lynette said, "Jazmin starts Monday. I'm looking forward to us working together. I heard from Jackson. He and Teresa are settling into their new place. Oh, and they found out the baby's sex. It's a girl."

"A son and a daughter. Perfect," said Susan. "Just like our family. I hope Ian gets along with his sister as well as you and Evan get along."

"Mom, you seem to have forgotten how much Evan and I bickered when we were growing up. And how mad I used to get when he tried to tag along with me and my friends. Oh, and the time Evan threw a TV at me."

Mike said, "But look at the two of you now. All grown up."

Jonathan pulled the curtains aside. "The minister is here. Let's get the show on the road so we can pop open the champagne."

ABOUT THE AUTHOR

Diane Weiner, award-winning author of The Susan Wiles Schoolhouse Mysteries, The Sugarbury Falls Mysteries, and The Sara Baron Tuned-in Mysteries, is a veteran public school teacher and mother of four grown children. Fond memories of reading Nancy Drew and Mary Higgins Clark mysteries on snowy weekends in upstate New York inspired her to write books that would bring that kind of joy to others. Being an animal lover, she is a vegetarian and shares her home with two precious cats—a calico named Callie and a gray tabby, Chelsea. In her free time, she enjoys running, shopping, attending theater productions, watching British mysteries on Britbox, and spending time with her family. To learn more about the author, visit her website www.dianeweinerauthor.com, or follow her on Facebook (dianeweinerauthor), Amazon, Goodreads, and Bookbub. Contact the author at dianeweinerauthor@gmail.com.